SPICY BITES

MACHINES

2022

ROMANCE
WRITERS
of Australia

Machines 2022 Spicy Bites Anthology

Anthology of Short Stories published by Romance Writers of Australia

Inc © 2022

eBook format: 978-0-6452177-3-5

Print format: 978-0-6452177-4-2

Spicy Bites Coordinator: Annette M Laarakkers

Cover design by Kim Lambert – Dreamstone Publishing

Edited by Anne Erskine

Formatting by Kim Lambert

OTHER SPICY BITES ANTHOLOGIES

Tattoo - 2017

Chains - 2018

Masks - 2019

Leather – 2020

Denim - 2021

SPICY BITES

MACHINES

Short Story Anthology

2022

VICTORIA BROWN

FIONA M MARSDEN

DK HARRIS

JENNIFER WESTGARTH

KAREN LIEVERSZ

LOUISA DUVAL

GEORGIA MOORE

KRISTIN SILK

KATRINA LOUISE

BRIDGET W DEEN

K.E. TURNER

CONTENTS

FOREWORD

Hot and heavy, dark and dangerous, or sleek and sophisticated. What is it that makes machines so sexy?

Prepare to find out in these twelve hot and sexy short stories centred around machines of all types.

We have so many talented authors that are part of the Romance Writers of Australia, and every year these anthologies just keep getting better, every year the choices just keep being harder. I am so proud of all the hard work that our members put in to these stories each and every year, and I just know you will enjoy everything you will find in these pages.

Buckle up and prepare to enjoy our 2022 Spicy Bites Anthology – Machines

Tracey Rosen

President

Romance Writers of Australia

I

LOVE, LUST AND V8'S

VICTORIA BROWN

G abby Pollard rang the front door bell of her sister's Fremantle home after the three-hour drive from the wheatbelt, wondering why she'd decided to go to the fifteen-year school reunion. It had seemed like a good idea at the time.

The door flew open and Bev pulled her into a hug. "Glad you *finally* made it."

"Sorry. Last minute emergency. You know a vet's work is never done."

Her brother-in-law Graham, niece Cindy and nephew Craig greeted her as they walked into the kitchen/diner.

Bev pulled out a chair. "Sit."

"Why? What are you doing?"

"I've planned this nerd-revenge for ages. You took the prize for it at school, Miss Super Studious." Bearing her renowned devil's grin, she yanked a cap over her sister's head.

"But I *never* colour my hair. And the reunion starts in two hours."

Bev shoved a lemonade in front of her. "Surely it's worth *some* effort."

She gulped down the drink.

An hour later, with her head feeling like a pin cushion, the cap was ripped off. "Ow! Did you leave any hair?"

Bev chuckled and beckoned her to lean over the laundry basin to rinse it.

Back in the chair, her sister's scissors rasped in anticipation. "How long since it's been cut? It's so old fashioned. This *is* the nineties, you know."

"Not sure. I've been super busy since I bought Jim's practice."

She looked down and gasped. "And why are your thighs hairy?"

"I've *never* shaved them. Geez!"

"You are so slack. Pride in oneself sis."

"Got better things to do." She slumped in the chair.

Bev cut and blow-dried Gabby's hair, then thrust a mirror at her.

What the hell? "You've gone all blonde on me."

"Your only defence against those premature greys."

"Thanks... Maybe?"

"Now what are you wearing?"

"I, er, didn't have time to get to the shops, so black pants? But I brought a pretty top."

"You're not going to Court." Bev huffed, caking Gabby's face in all manner of 'stuff'.

It felt like drying clay about to set rock-hard. Then came mascara, eye shadow and lipstick, usually reserved for weddings and funerals only. She gaped at the alien forming in the mirror. "This is not me!"

"Think of it as an extension of yourself."

They were about to leave when Cindy reappeared. "Wow. You look lovely, especially in Mum's dress and stilettos."

Gabby nearly poked her tongue at her niece, having rarely worn a dress in the last dozen years, and *never* a flouncy, pastel, floral with shoestring straps. "It's too short. I'll be pulling it down all night. But when I do, my boobs come out. And I'm going to topple in these heels and tower over everybody.' She glared at Bev. "How did I let you talk me into this?"

Bev winked. "Hope you get to pull the dress *up* some time. Speaking of which, is Mark going?"

"No idea."

"Hmm. Me thinks that's the only reason you came." Adding in soprano, "Memmmooriees."

"Of noisy V8's, rock music and wild times. Not Mark!"

"Yeah right." Bev grabbed the keys and called out to her husband, "Back in a minute, dear." She turned to her sister. "I'm dropping you off so you can have some fun. When was your last hangover?"

They pulled into the car park of the Fremantle Function Centre and Gabby leaned across and pecked her sister's cheek, feeling slutty and overdone but renewed just the same. "Thanks for this."

"No worries. And I don't want to see you till tomorrow. Didn't go to all this trouble for nothing. Here's a spare key."

⚮

Entering the large, packed room of blaring music and dulled lights, Gabby tugged at the sides of the dress and headed for the drinks stand.

As she neared it, heads turned and a theatrical screech rang out. "Gabrielle Pollard? Is that you?"

It was Karen, leader of her class's bitchy gang, who took her into a hug. "Great to see you."

Gabby stiffened and winced. "You too."

The rest of that gang joined them and chatted, all welcoming and friendly. How odd. And everyone who came to the drinks stand gaped at her. She grinned. Best revenge-of-the-nerds ever. *Bev will be pleased.*

Gulping her fourth drink, talking and laughing — louder by the drink — her eyes involuntarily roamed the room — admitting to her subconscious-self that she *had* only come in the hope of seeing Mark. What an idiot. They were never serious. He was always going overseas as soon as his mechanical apprenticeship finished and she was cavernously deep into her veterinary studies. Friends with benefits, that was all. Sadly, she'd received only one postcard from London, a month after he flew out. Then nothing. For thirteen years.

"Looking for Mark?"

The question made her jump. "Noooo."

Karen smirked. "Well, you need to tell your eyes that. They haven't stopped casing the joint. You two were like the perfect pair set for life. None of us could believe he just up and left."

Ouch. Yep. Same Karen.

Pointing to a dark corner, Karen continued, "Over there. He's not long walked in."

Gabby's heart lurched. Mark stood out at six foot two. More muscled now and his sandy hair neater than she remembered. The tight-fitting jeans and shirt were certifiably gobsmacking. Their eyes locked. *Shit!* Questioning lines crossed his brow before a smile graced his lips. He excused himself and headed toward her.

Jelly legs melted her to the spot. Her vibrating cup spilled. She dumped it on the table, frantically inhaling and exhaling as he neared. Licking her parched lips, she gulped.

"Hullo," he uttered in the same deep, sexy tone she remembered.

"Hi Mark," the other girls chanted, almost choir-like with overly-plucked eyebrows jiggling at different rates.

He appeared not to have heard as he stared, his expression that of a startled goldfish.

She begged her body to disappear through the floor, but the stupid high heels formed an impenetrable barrier.

"Gabby? Is that really you?"

Clearing her throat, despite there being nothing stuck in it, she managed, "Gidday mate," — their old greeting. "No. Not me. Sister Bev's creation."

He chuckled and nudged her arm. "Wanna dance?"

Abandoned by her voice, she nodded.

His hand slipped easily into hers, as if it had never left. Large and calloused but warm. When they reached the dance floor, he let go. Her hand tried to keep hold. *What the hell?* Late seventies songs drummed through her ears. Was this a conspiracy? She battled to bring her eyes up to meet his, feeling them piercing a direct route to her heart and below in sync as he bobbed to the music.

Leaning in close he whispered, "I'm glad you came."

Her face turned into a furnace. Hopefully masked by the plaster-thick foundation. Were her neck and ears giving her away? With conversation restricted by the music, she glanced and smiled at him intermittently and awkwardly.

Then a slow song came on. He opened his arms and thirteen years melted away as she slotted into them. Her head nestled on his shoulder, his breath warmed her hair and spicy aftershave made her tingle. A broad hand supported the small of her back. His fast-beating heart resonated through her chest, in rhythm with hers. Mark. Best friend and best benefits ever. With legs entwined, they swayed in harmony, moulded like warmed chocolate, until the song ended. Far too soon.

Back at the drinks stand, the bitchy, sort-of-turned-nice group homed in on him and chatted.

"Another drink?" Gabby asked, desperate for more alcohol to tame the idiocy happening within her.

"Yes please. Just a light beer. I'm driving."

Back with the group, she passed Mark the drink.

"Thanks." He leaned in close.

Her bourbon nearly went flying. *Get a grip.*

"Can we split when you've finished that?"

She nodded, her heart surged, and down below partied. She skulled the drink.

∞

With the warm night air and full-moon shining — and not to mention being whacked by alcohol — Gabby swanned alongside Mark feeling light as a puffy cloud. They reached a ute sign-written, "Mobile Mechanic."

"Still working on cars?"

"Sure am. It's my own business."

His proud grin as he opened her door nearly tipped her off the heels. She quickly fell into the seat.

"Sorry it's no flashy beast with a roaring V8. Not practical."

"Same here. Mine's a boring four-wheel drive wagon these days."

"Can't imagine that." He turned toward the beach. "I heard on the grapevine you were with a farmer from the wheatbelt and got a job near him."

"Oh. Derek. A seven-year relationship till a pretty, female year-three teacher arrived and rumours started. Small town and all."

"You poor girl."

"Not really. It was hard at first. I couldn't leave town because I'd bought the practice. I have to admit, the spark between those two is something we never really had. They're getting married next year. She's lovely."

"He didn't drive a throbbing V8 then?"

"No. Crumby four-cylinder tray-back. Into sheep not machines that boy. I mean, I love sheep, but..."

"What about other farmers with V8 Utes?"

Gabby sighed. "Ooooh. Those sexy cars. Lowered, loud, fat bull-bars decked with phallic aerials. I love the donuts and figures-of-eight they can do. I call it paddock ballet."

Mark chuckled.

"What a turn on. Oops." She giggled and tapped two fingers to her mouth in a stop-the-rot motion. "Sorry. Booze brain. I dated some, but nothing serious."

"Fell for their cars more than them?"

"Probably."

As she turned to him grinning, a shimmering flicker of gold on his left hand caught her eye. The smile vanished. A wedding ring? *What on earth?* Why hadn't she noticed it earlier? *Drunken idiot.*

"Gabby. I'm really sorry. One postcard in thirteen years. That's unforgiveable." He squirmed with his eyes glued to the road. "You see..."

She wafted a hand, her brain fogging with shock and heart dripping with disappointment. "Don't worry. We agreed remember? And were never anything more than..." She stopped, mesmerised by the ring. Unfinished sentences? Just like their relationship. Her head spun and it wasn't just from the alcohol. "Would you mind dropping me back to Bev's?"

"Already? Um. I thought maybe we could cruise the beaches. Get a burger. Like the old days. You hungry?"

Her stomach grumbled. There'd been no time for dinner with operation-reform-Gabby. "Yes."

"And I really need to explain." He glanced at her with a determined expression.

She raised a hand in protest. "Mark. Honestly..."

He interrupted. "Actually. I've got a better idea." The car swung with a U-turn away from the beach and ten minutes later he parked in front of an older house on a large block. "Hop out and wait here."

Gabby did so, noticing an extra driveway leading to a shed at the rear. Lights were on inside. Her anger rose. How rude of him not to introduce her to his wife. *Sleaze.* Or was she too embarrassingly drunk? Probably too slutty looking. *What's taking so long?* Shuffle. Shuffle. Waver. *Oops. Don't fall over.* Was he trying to convince his wife that she, mystery-woman-in-the-driveway didn't matter? *A fact, princess.*

A familiar rumble broke the cursing. Her heart jolted. A V8? Then... *Oh my God.* The reversing panel van thumped its way toward her. Deep satin blue, with highly polished chrome on the exhaust, coffin rack on the roof, wheels and bumpers. The 1976 Sandman he'd modified glistened in the moonlight.

Even now, in 1992, it was a stand-out legend. Her pulse hit warp-speed as a tidal wave of memories, emotions and sexual rumblings bombarded her at once. What was happening between her legs needed censoring.

A child's cry broke her musings. *Got kids as well? Double sleaze.*

Mark parked, leapt out and bounced around to the passenger door. "Hop in," he beamed, gesturing.

With her heart thumping like the V8, she tried to cement herself to the pavement. Too many memories. Too much water under the bridge. *No. No. NO!*

But the van beckoned her like a powerful magnet. From another lifetime. A crazy, fun and sexually exciting era. *Oh. What the hell.* She melted into the bucket seat, soaking up its familiar leather scent with a deep breath. Ripping the stilettos off, she stretched her legs as Mark jumped behind the wheel.

"I can't believe you kept it," she grinned.

Reversing out he grinned back at her.

At the first corner he glanced around — clearly watching out for cops — and planted his foot.

The engine roared and as the van took off, the force threw her back. "Oh. Wow. I'd forgotten how good that feels." It thundered toward South Beach, its resonating exhaust and pounding eight cylinders vibrating the seat, awakening long-forgotten senses. She squirmed as her girly bits sprung to life.

Then a profound realisation whacked her. A light bulb moment. No wonder farmer Derek's interest in her had waned, and they had never felt that spark. She was *bed boring* with a capital B. Sexually programmed to hot machines only. A car fetishist.

But then the Ute owners hadn't advanced much past first base in the arousal stakes. Crammed with farm gear in the back and needing to be a yoga pro to complete any acts in the front, they were definitely not in the same league. Maybe it was a panel van fetish. Her now burning crotch felt as if it had stirred from a deep coma, like Sleeping Beauty. Squirming, Gabby shook her head. *Married. Remember?*

Mark cleared his throat, startling her. "Before I turn up the stereo, I need to get this off my chest."

"Okay." *Chest?* Her mind floated back to the silky feel of his naturally hairless set of abs. *Geez.* The sexual sparks were making *her* feel like the cheating slime-ball.

"Again. I'm so sorry."

"Please, stop apologising."

Instinctively, she went to place a reassuring palm on his thigh, where it had always rested, and quickly pulled back. She glanced over. Memories sparked, of her hand moving up the thigh to his lap and circling his crotch until it bulged. Releasing his damn, large, super hard cock. Encasing its prominent head, squeezing up and down its length as whopping surges begged her to satisfy its need. Daring fingers creeping lower, cupping his testicles. Leaning over and smoothing moistened lips along and around his length, loving the silkiness. The tip of her tongue spreading its opening.

Gabby licked her lips, almost tasting him, feeling the pulses that always gushed between her legs in time with the throb of Mark and his machine. Her lower regions were almost exploding. *Oh man. Don't stop the car.*

"Are you thinking what I'm thinking?"

His voice snapped her back to reality. She blinked and stiffened. "What? What?"

"The things we used to do."

Crossing her legs and feeling her cheeks flare *again*, she snickered, "Guilty as charged."

He laughed. "The drive-ins, bog laps around Fremantle, burn outs and dragging cars." Then pouted. "Your Holden always beat me. Man, it was fast."

Oh. *Those* thoughts. Reminder. Married. *You're in a strictly friend-zone, girl.* She sighed, deflating like a balloon, instructing her aroused body that this was a burger-and-cruise-down-memory-lane escapade only. "It's a wonder we're still alive."

Her mind wandered back to the adrenalin rushes and sexual highs. Lights coming on at the Drive-ins while they were still busy in the back. Sex acts while speeding down the highway — thank God for automatics — and parked in public places. Her favourite front clasping bras. Mark's panel van. Best times and best bed ever. Well, living with their individual parents at the time, the only bed.

Stop!

Gabby gulped. "Reckon I had more sex, alcohol and broke more road rules in those few years than in the next thirteen. What happened to those days?"

He shrugged. "Life, I guess. We grew up."

"Better change the subject. This conversation, your panel van. They're doing all sorts of silly things to me." Her drunken mouth blurted. *What the hell?* "Sorry."

"Why be sorry?" His eyebrows flicked up and down as he snuck a glance her way.

It didn't make sense. He was always Mr Upright-Principles-Plus. The bottom end of the cheating spectrum. Had Mark's scruples flown overseas with him?

He cleared his throat. "I really need to explain."

"No, you don't." She thrust her palm his direction. "We agreed, there was to be no more *us* when you got on that plane. And that there never really was a serious *us*."

"Except I wasn't completely honest." His brows furrowed. "I, er, wanted you to join me. I knew you couldn't because of your studies. And once you qualified... well. Your life would take you elsewhere. It broke my heart but I had to leave you. And going overseas was the best way."

Gabby swallowed. "Why didn't you tell me?"

"It wouldn't have changed anything. At first, I followed my mate around London like a miserable street dog. He had to help me make your postcard sound happy. Admittedly, writing and I don't get on."

"I gathered that."

He smiled and patted her knee.

Shit! It set it on fire. Memories flooded in of his beefy left hand caressing her thigh while he drove. Crawling higher. Smoothing over her crotch. Round and round. Her tingling with the touch. His fingers sourcing the lip of her skirt and carefully weaving their way under it. Then seeking the rim of her knickers and edging between her legs. Them parting; begging for him to explore.

The throbbing of the motor, pounding music. Her breath catching. Squirming in the seat with her crotch on fire. The tip of his fore finger dancing delicate pirouettes on her clit. Her gasping, inhaling and holding her breath. Pulsing. Pulsing. Two fingers creeping lower, finding their mark and edging inside. Shimmying forward to accommodate them. Send them deeper. Ecstasy rising and falling in never ending waves. Cries of delight.

Stop! He's married. You are not having an affair, fling, thoughtie, whatever, with a married man. Gabby writhed and stared out her window. *Damn you, car!*

His voice made her jump. "A few months later, I met an Irish lady, Carrie, and we travelled Europe for a while. I still wanted to keep in touch with you, but I couldn't. I chickened out."

"It's okay. Really."

"Phew. I'm forgiven then?" He wiped his brow. But she noticed the relief was brief. His face contorted into a wrinkled ball as his eyes glued to the road and hands trembled somewhat on the wheel.

She felt the urge to steady them as he hesitated. For quite a while. What Pandora's box had she opened? "I get that you're a married, family man."

"What? Why would you think that?"

"A child cried at your house."

"That's my nephew. My sister, Kelly, left her abusive husband and moved in with her two boys."

"But what about this?" She tapped the ring, expecting it to sear her like a hot, cheating poker.

A long, awkward silence filled the cab.

Finally, Mark sighed and continued, "Carrie moved here from Ireland. We married and a couple of years later tried to have kids. But nothing happened." He paused and she saw his Adam's apple bob. "They found cancer in her uterus. After a long illness, she died. Three years ago."

Gabby's hand shot to her mouth. "You poor man. I'm so sorry. I had no idea."

He rolled the ring around with his right hand, blinking. "I can't take this off." His eyes looked moist, and his pleading glance seemed to be asking for help.

She patted his arm, which sent shivers down hers. *Damn it.* "You don't have to."

"I poured myself into the business after that. Needless to say, it's booming. But since Kelly and the boys moved in a year ago, I've been much better. She's awesome and I love playing Dad."

"Good to hear."

He drummed the steering wheel and glanced at her, still bleary-eyed, but with a weak smile gracing his quivering lips. "It's the first time I've driven this baby since Carrie died. Had to jump start the poor girl."

"No wonder you were gone a while." Her heart swelled to a basketball "Wow. I bet your sister was glad to hear it."

"Yep. Apart from waking the kids."

His expression was peaceful now.

And Gabby's grin so broad, she felt the foundation crack.

A half-hour later, they parked at the burger van at Cottesloe beach. The night was warm and still as they waited for their order.

"Be back in a minute. Just going to the loo," Gabby said.

The ride had turned her on so much, the toilet paper whooshed away at warp-speed. Washing her hands, she stared at the lottery-winning, giggly teenager beaming back at her in the mirror.

Mark grabbed the burgers, high-revved the van to the nearest beach, parked and switched off the motor.

She wound down the window, mesmerised by the Indian ocean shimmering in the moonlight. Breathing in the salty air and tuning-in to the gentle lapping of the waves on the shore, she took his left hand and rested it on her bare thigh. His caress was so light it made the fine leg hairs stand on end and her skin try to soak it up like a magical moisturizer.

Moving close, his spicy aftershave teased her nostrils and had her wanting more. His lips were instantly on hers, melting thirteen years away. Still gentle, yet sizzling. Powerful as ever. Setting her more on fire. If that were possible.

He pulled away and whispered. "That's to say 'sorry'." And kissed her again. This time his tongue tip tempted her lips apart. "That says, 'I'm glad you were at the reunion'." The next was a slow waltz of entwined tongues. "That's a 'thank you for getting me driving the panel van again'." Before Gabby could respond, his lips pressed hard, hungry and rampant this time, tongue deep and exploring. A fast, seductive tango leaving her breathless. He broke away tweaking his eyebrows. "Wanna hop in the back for old time's sake?"

Not quickly enough. She snickered and nodded — on the outside. Inside she was blazing.

"I'll just find a more private spot."

"That never used to bother you."

"I know. Old and sober." He drove to the bushy corner of the carpark and reversed in this time. Thump. Thump. Thump. Then turned off the motor and cranked the stereo. The glorious tones of ELO's 'Livin Thing,' filled the van.

"Oh My God! You remembered our song."

His grin set her whole body alight.

After opening the tailgate, they dived in, barely getting the folded sheet spread, that he must have grabbed from the house. Mark pulled her on top, frantically kissing her, while his firm hands smoothed over her bum cheeks. Tingly tremors shot through every cell as she pressed and writhed against his crotch. He slid her knickers down while she fumbled with the buttons on his shirt. Then he rolled away and shucked his jeans. Her electrified hands ran under his jocks, desperate for the feel of that super hard, large, silky and *hot, hot,* cock. Some things are never forgotten.

"Oh man. It's like I'm twenty again. This car. You. Amazing."

"I'm still pinching myself Gabs. The things you did to me." His hand ran between her legs and the fore and middle fingers found their mark.

She clenched her thighs around them, zinging all over.

The full-moon, sexy van, throbbing music, memories. Their lips glued. Fingers deep and tantalising. Heat from his throbbing cock. The frantic build-up. A frenzy. *Nooo. Don't peak. Not yet. Not yet.* Gabby removed her hand and he did the same.

Then he eased on top of her. Skin on seething skin sliding and gyrating, with Mark as powerful, gentle and loving, as ever.

And her barely able to breathe.

Adding a condom, he slowly sank deep inside, pulsing and thrusting perfectly in rhythm with her. *Oh my God.* They crescendoed with the music and when the last song of the CD ended, her screams and his roar shattered the still night air.

"Wow. I'd forgotten how good car sex..."

Her words were squashed by his lips, tender and warm as he held her close.

After they'd been lying entwined for a while, an approaching car's lights shone in.

"S'pose we'd better get dressed. Our burgers'll be pretty cold." He grinned.

Begging time to stand still, Gabby gathered her clothes.

At one o'clock, pulling up at Bev's house, Mark kissed her. "Can I take you on a proper date? Spend the night? We never got to do that."

She sighed. "I'm supposed to stay with the folks tonight. And I've gotta be back Sunday." Her heart lodged a protest. Between her legs a full-on riot broke out. "S'pose they'll understand."

His eyes flashed as he grinned. "Great. Pick you up at five?"

"It's a date, mate." She pecked his cheek and got out feeling featherlight and floaty, as if she was on a cloud.

As the panel van crept away, her eyes stayed glued to the sexy machine until it disappeared around the corner.

❦

"Rise and shine."

Gabby squinted at Bev's blurry outline on the edge of the bed.

"So. Was Mark there?"

"Yep. And sexier than ever. He's still got the panel van. Can you believe it?" Gabby flicked her eyebrows. "Last night we..."

Bev blocked her ears. "Ew. You and cars. I couldn't think of anything worse."

"He's asked me out tonight. Do you think Mum and Dad'll mind?"

Bev thought for a moment. "I'll invite them for lunch instead. They'll be fine."

"Thank you, sis. Better get a wriggle on then."

At five o'clock, after a wonderful family get-together, her heart flipped hearing the rumble of the approaching van. Opening the door to Mark, she held back a gasp. He looked as sexy as hell in the close-fitting, long-legged black shorts and a blue patterned shirt which brought out the azure of his eyes. Her breath hitched as he kissed her cheek before greeting the others.

She grabbed the overnight bag, hugged the family, whispered, "Thanks," to Bev and raced out the door like a teenager.

"Take me away," she laughed as the van fired into life. With her hand on his thigh, Gabby got that floating feeling again. Cloud Nine? Cloud ninety-nine more like.

Mark glanced at her. "I still can't believe it. You. This car."

"Me neither."

As he roared along the streets familiar feelings of freedom, peace and excitement fired through her veins — together with hot, sexual surges. Bolts of wanting. She tried to chat about inane, thirteen year-gap-filling stuff, but battled to focus. The engine's throbbing resonated between her legs making her groin sizzle and her hand on his thigh singed. A lethal combination begging him to park.

After an hour he asked, "You hungry?"

"Yes. But not for food." She tweaked her eyebrows and grinned.

He merely laughed, turned toward the coast and parked at the Shorefront Hotel.

No car sex tonight? The disappointment sent her inner parts from boiling to a low simmer.

അ

Gabby gazed out the window of the top floor suite. The Indian Ocean glistened and the lightly clouded sky filled with a mix of mauves and pinks from the setting sun. With the spa filling, Mark came up behind her, peppering kisses on her neck. Each one sent little shivers down her spine to her groin, upping the simmering a notch. She turned and stared momentarily before meeting his lips and scorching tongue. His roaming hands set her skin alight.

She pushed against his bulging crotch as he eased the t-shirt over her head. Then she ripped his shirt off, her hands smoothing over his shiny, muscled chest.

In slow motion, he unzipped her shorts and let them fall to the floor. His hand caressed her groin with a featherlight touch.

She pressed hard against it in response, before pulling back and yanking her undies off — desperate for the feel of his exploring fingers, groaning as they found their mark. Hauling his jocks off, she gripped his smooth, hard cock, sighing loudly.

"Spa should be ready," he gasped, easing away and leading her to it.

She looked at their entwined hands because something felt different. The ring was gone.

He followed her gaze and pulled her close, for a long, deep and tender kiss. "That one's 'Thanks. It's in the box with Carrie's where it belongs'."

Her heart melted.

He sat in the middle of the spa and she straddled him. The warm bubbles dancing about intensified her already sizzling body.

His unhurried palm circled over her left breast, a finger and thumb gently tweaking the nipple. Leaning down, he rolled his tongue over it. Then brought his head up, sprinkling her neck with kisses and teasing her right ear lobe. His two hands grasped each side of her thigh and pulled her up to stand over him.

Gabby drew in an enormous breath as his hot, wet tongue and lips teased her clit and toyed with the surrounding folds. Every nerve ending pinged from small nips of this teeth. It felt like a thousand sparklers were going off inside her. She clenched handfuls of his hair, breathless as he worked his magic. Euphoric ripples grew to a tsunami of waves and tremors and with a final explosion she yelled, "Mark. Oh my God!" And collapsed into the bubbles, heaving, rejoicing and hugging him tight.

The proud grin lighting his handsome face, took her breath away.

They dried each other with slow, tender strokes and fell on the bed moulded as one from head to toe. Mark pulled away, rolled on a condom and crept on top. Still kissing, he eased inside her with unhurried, deep thrusts.

Each contraction and release of her muscles clamped his length, massing her with goosebumps. No thinking, only feeling. So beautiful. So satisfying. So perfect. Another orgasm pulsed through her and with a booming holler, he joined her final release.

She lay in his arms taking in slow, easy breaths, relishing the afterglow.

Mark kissed her cheek and whispered, "You know. I only came to the reunion hoping you'd be there. To rekindle what we had."

Her heart surged. "Think I did the same."

His grin spread for a mile.

Gabby's did too with a realisation. This wasn't any car fetish she'd had all these years.

Not even a panel van fetish.

It was a Mark fetish.

2

VINTAGE LOVE MACHINES

LOUISA DUVAL

Dwayne

I stared at Fergie Jones running buck naked through the waist-high cosmos flowers of Thompson's Field. My jeans, keys and tee shirt were in her left hand, her clothes and a Massey Ferguson steering wheel in her right.

She reached her ute, pulled on her shirt and skirt and took off, leaving me with a ten-minute walk of shame back to Ballydoon with my wallet, hat, socks and boots, and a crankshaft for a 1927 Fordson F tractor.

With a sock strategically covering Dwayne Junior, I walked quickly past the general store, my hat down.

"Nice buns, Dwayne!" someone catcalled. Yikes, it was Beryl Rasmussen, Ballydoon's eighty-year-old hornbag. I picked up my pace and strode into Turner's Mechanical less than a minute later.

"Dwayne Moline," my boss, Bruce Turner, boomed. "Where the heck are your clothes? And your car?"

"Fergie stole my keys and clothes. Had to leave my ute behind," I muttered. My fellow mechanic, Ryan, sniggered. "Luckily my wallet fell out of my jeans before she drove off."

"How on earth did Fergie steal your clothes?" Ryan asked, eyes wide. "Did you *sleep* with her trying to get the steering wheel for the Golden Grey?"

"No! Course not." I let the crankshaft clatter on the workbench as I pulled a purple flower from my hair. "No."

What should have been a civil exchange of vintage tractor parts at Thompson's Field between bitter rivals had instead been...

My cheeks flushed red hot.

I'd ended up near naked, buried between Fergie's thighs.

How could my nemesis taste so good? Fergie should've tasted like coffee and toothpaste or coriander. But she'd tasted like sunshine, fresh sheets and raspberries.

What the hell? I was writing poetry in my mind now about Fergie?

I dropped the purple flower and took my hat off, covering up Dwayne Junior. Thoughts of her writhing against my tongue, tugging my hair and moaning my name had my blood heading south again.

I frowned. Had Fergie attempted to seduce me to get the Fordson crankshaft she needed for her tractor entry in the Vintage Farm Machinery Restoration category at the Stanmore Agricultural Show?

If she had, her plans failed. Even if she did have my clothes, and keys. And received a goddamn great orgasm.

"Well, it's war," I declared. "I'm going to win at the show with my Grey. Did she stop by here?"

Bruce shook his head. "Goddammit, Dwayne," he sighed.

"Quit covering your junk with your hat and get dressed."

My tractor glowed in the middle of the workshop as I headed to my locker.

"But Fergie still has the F35 steering wheel you need," Ryan pointed out as I pulled on my spare jeans. "How do you suppose you're going to get it now?"

"Only one thing to do." I pulled on a tee-shirt with a Turner's Racing logo. "Seduce her for it."

Two can play at this game, Ferg.

"Oh, geez." Bruce muttered, looking to the ceiling while Ryan shook his head.

"What?"

"Since high school, you two have been unbearable," Ryan said, holding up his fingers. "You both tied for the manual arts subject prize. You restored a vintage motorbike, Fergie did a 1963 Mini Cooper. Then you had to do one better by restoring the Ford ute. And now, it's tractors."

"Kid stuff." I waved a hand, scoffing. "It's always been about vintage tractors. I bought the Grey in Year Eleven."

"Yes. A Massey Ferguson tractor," Bruce drawled.

"So?" I shrugged. "It's a classic."

They both groaned.

"Her name is Fergie," Bruce said slowly.

"I'm well aware," I frowned again.

Bruce pinched the bridge of his nose. "What happened that led to you two feuding over tractors?"

I remembered all too well. Spin the Bottle at a party in Year Nine. When it was my turn, the bottle had landed on her. Her impossibly soft lips had parted in surprise. My heart had hammered out a racket against my ribs.

"She's hated me since Year Nine." I swallowed hard. "Told everyone she'd rather eat dirt than kiss me. No idea why I was so repulsive."

"You can't be that repulsive if you ended up naked today," Ryan grinned.

I shrugged. My cheeks were burning. Today, she'd sung my praises to the clouds as I brought her to climax amongst the purple and pink flowers. Fergie had demanded, begged and encouraged me to kiss her everywhere. But, we hadn't kissed on the lips.

I also wasn't about to tell my co-workers that after she'd orgasmed, Fergie had ordered me to lie on my back and close my eyes. I'd done so, my dick pointing to the sky.

Next thing I'd heard the muffled clink of my keys. I'd opened my eyes to find her running across the field naked, hightailing it through the flowers, leaving me with an erection that wouldn't quit.

If she had intended to seduce me so she could steal the ninety-five-year-old crankshaft for her Fordson, Fergie hadn't taken that vital tractor part she needed.

"Damn vixen of a woman." I held out my hand. "Can I use a loaner car to get my stuff?"

"Not just your stuff," Bruce sighed, dangling the keys for the garage's hatchback over my palm. "I'm lending you the car so you sort this thing out between you both, once and for all."

"What do you mean, 'this thing'?"

"Bloody hell, Dwayne, talk to her. Maybe, just maybe, there's something going on between you two that's more than tractors."

Fergie

I picked up Dwayne's tee shirt. It smelled of cologne, sweat, and a hint of engine oil. I moaned before I realised I'd sniffed his clothes.

I was losing my mind.

My fickle mind strayed back to how he'd growled when I'd pulled off his shirt over his head, leaving scratches across his chest. And how I'd flicked my tongue over my fingernail marks to soothe him.

And when he'd kissed me between my legs and then swirled his tongue, his attention could only be described as *feasting* on me. He'd lapped and sucked and I'd begged him to keep going, screaming his name so loud a flock of cockatoos took flight, screeching along with me.

Heat built up low in my belly.

How had swapping a steering wheel for a crankshaft turned into both of us ripping off each other's clothes and me orgasming under a clear, blue sky as pink and mauve flowers danced in the breeze?

Panic welled up again. I let his shirt drop to the counter.

"Hey Ferg, Dad said he'll be in later to do this repair on Pam's car." My sister, Vicki, walked into Jones Mechanical garage dressed for work at the aged care home, carrying a box marked 'Pam's Falcon 1998 right mirror'. "Did you get the crankshaft from your arch enemy?"

No, I got the Big O instead.

I blushed, shaking my head.

"Why can't you just talk to Dwayne like a civilised human being?"

I ignored her.

Ever since she'd started seeing Matt, owner of the chocolate shop near Ballydoon, Vicki shipped romance whenever a man and woman vaguely came near each other.

"You two have always been at each other's throats," my sister sighed, placing the box down on the counter.

Except when his face is between my thighs. At that thought, I fanned myself.

"Whose are they?" Vicki pointed at Dwayne's clothes.

"No one's." I hastily dumped his stuff into the box. "Rags for work."

My sister picked up a set of keys. "These are Dwayne's, aren't they?" The Turner's Mechanical key ring swung in front of my face, mocking me. "Oh my god, what did you do?"

"I had the best orgasm of my life." I slumped over the counter. *And I've been wondering how I could have another as soon as possible.*

"You had sex with Dwayne over tractor parts?"

"Yes, no. Sort of." I looked up. "Vick, he went down on me, and it was so good. And he really liked it, too."

My sister squealed. "You had hate sex!"

"What? Noooo."

Maybe?

"So, you like him now?"

The difference between like versus hate was now very confusing.

"Dwayne proposed a truce by swapping the steering wheel he needs for his Golden Grey with the Fordson crankshaft I need and I agreed to meet."

I didn't want a truce. I didn't like him at all.

But I had liked how I'd caught him staring at my legs, his eyes travelling up my body like he'd realised for the first time I was a woman. His eyes had locked on mine — the usual look of irritation mixed with lust and want.

I had yanked on his shirt hard just so I could taste his skin where his neck joined his shoulder. He'd snarled like a feral dog. Next was a blur. Suddenly our shirts were off, next his boots and jeans, and then he was naked. I'd pushed him to the ground and kept on licking him all over and then I was flipped on my back, staring at the sky, my shirt gone, and his mouth pressed right *there*.

"Geez, is it hot in here?" I panted.

After that orgasm, I had no idea what was up and what was down.

"You *like* him," Vicki sang with a smug grin.

"I liked *it*, the orgasm. I don't like *him*." I paused, taking a deep breath. "I'm closing the garage now and driving back to Ballydoon to return his clothes and keys. And then, that's that. Never see him again."

"Wait a big, fat, long second." Vicki planted her hand on her hip, raising an eyebrow. "Where did the sexing go down? You were meant to meet at a neutral location."

"Thompsons Field," I mumbled.

Vicki squealed again. "Outdoor hate sex! And then, you stole his clothes and keys? That's just mean."

"I panicked." I winced. "I just grabbed everything and took off."

"Why?" she demanded.

"I don't know," I wailed, throwing up my hands.

"So, what? No more seeing him? No more tractor feuds? No more orgasms?"

I scrubbed my face.

Oh, how I wanted more orgasms.

A throat cleared behind me. "Um, excuse me, Fergie?"

My sister's eyes lit up. I knew that deep voice without having to turn around, but I did anyway.

"Dwayne."

"I, ah, came to get my things. Then I'll be on my way."

My sister scuttled past, dumping his keys in my hands, and grabbing two things nearest to her.

"I'm just—" She held up a crowbar and a stapler. "I need these. For work. In aged care. Badly. Okay. Goodbye now."

She left in a flash via the back door, leaving me to face my nemesis.

ᎃᏋᏁ᎒

Dwayne

I strode towards her, clutching the 1927 Fordson F crankshaft, ready to deliver a speech I'd rehearsed during the twenty-minute drive from Ballydoon to Jones Mechanical in Stanmore.

But Fergie cut me off before I could say a word.

"What the hell did you do today with that tongue of yours?" Her tone was accusatory.

"I... what?" I frowned. "It's called oral sex—"

"I know what it's called." Fergie threw my keys onto the

counter and moved to stand before me. "I've had men do that before. But I've never... *you know*."

I arched an eyebrow. "No one's ever made you come like that before?"

"You were the first." Fergie slowly shook her head, her eyes roaming over my body.

My blood ran hot with pride that I'd done something for her no other man had.

Shit. Dwayne Junior was hard again.

Pride was a dangerous thing.

"Can you make me orgasm again?" Fergie's tone was part disbelief, part curious, like she didn't think I was capable of a repeat performance.

"Are you asking what I think you're asking?" I spluttered.

I should put this crankshaft down on the counter, get my things and leave.

Rehearsing my speech on the drive over had been difficult enough with how I kept remembering how sweet Fergie had tasted, laid out in a field of flowers.

But now, the way she was looking at me, all I could think about was how I was still hungry.

"Maybe today was a fluke."

"Oh Fergie, that was no fluke," I scoffed. "That was skill and paying attention."

She rolled her eyes. "Others have tried valiantly. You just got lucky."

"That right?" Fergie wasn't fooling either of us. Her orgasm had nothing to do with luck. I advanced, backing her up against the mudguard of her Fordson F tractor. "You want more?"

"Yes," she breathed.

As much as Dwayne Junior was insisting we get down to business right away, I had my own demand.

"I want more, too." Her breath hitched. "A kiss. You didn't kiss me in the field."

"Wh-what?" she blinked. "We kissed plenty times today."

"I don't mean your mouth on my neck or my chest. And I don't mean my mouth on your tits, Fergie. Or your thighs." My voice had dropped an octave. "Or your pussy."

Her cheeks pinked.

"You're begging me right now to give you more orgasms and we haven't even kissed. Trust me, I noticed."

Fergie stared at my lips and then licked her own. I almost lost my mind right there and then.

"We didn't?"

"No."

Our voices could barely be heard.

Her breasts brushed against my chest as she got up on tippy toes.

Holy shit. My speech... My brain had stopped working altogether. Her mouth was so close, and then she pressed her lips against mine.

So soft. Heaven.

I sighed, letting the crankshaft fall to the concrete floor with an almighty clang. We didn't so much as pause. Fergie speared her hands into my hair. Her tongue flicked once, then twice across my lips, teasing me to open up to her. I gave in. Our tongues tangled. My hands found her waist and then her butt, squeezing her flesh with a groan.

I couldn't touch enough of her.

All sense and reason fled Jones Mechanical, and probably the whole of Stanmore.

Who cared about tractors and vintage farm machinery competitions for the ag show?

Kissing Fergie Jones was my new obsession. Why hadn't we been kissing like this sooner?

She broke our kiss with a cry. "I need you."

I growled, as I nipped and sucked at her skin, making her squirm.

"More," she moaned, leaning back on the curve of the mudguard as she pulled up her shirt, exposing her breasts for the second time today, her nipples as red as raspberries.

I offered up a silent prayer of thanks to Ford engineering, taking as much of her breast as I could into my mouth, licking, sucking.

Ford had added the tapered mudguards to the 1927 Fordson model F tractor after complaints that the lightweight tractor was overbalancing and tipping backwards. Who knew these damn mudguards could arch her body perfectly so I could give her breasts all my attention?

And my colleagues had the cheek to say tractors weren't sexy.

Within a minute, her tee-shirt was on the floor and my hands were stroking her inner thighs and my blood was rushing in my ears and my cock was straining against my jeans.

Fergie cupped my jaw.

"Condom?"

"In wallet." I croaked.

"Thank god," she muttered. "Hurry, *please*."

I groaned, taking in the view. Fergie, lying against the tractor, those eyes of hers full of heat and longing. She'd rucked her skirt up and braced one leg against the other mudguard, her pussy completely bare to me, glistening wet.

"Jesus, Fergie. You were commando the whole time?"

"This is a sexual emergency of the highest order right now, Dwayne Moline," Fergie snapped. "Wallet. Now."

I freed my wallet from my back pocket and scrambled to undo my fly, setting a new world record for disrobing as my jeans and boxer briefs hit my ankles.

Fergie wrapped her hand around my aching dick and then gently stroked up and down.

"Christ, Fergie." I wrapped my hand around hers, stilling her. "If you want me to come inside you, you have to stop."

"Condom," she said, nodding vigorously.

She didn't let go though. She squeezed my dick in encouragement as I frantically emptied my wallet on the counter. Cash, cards, a band aid and — *that's where I put Mrs Marsden's new spark plug for her Toyota Corolla* — finally the condom fell out.

"Yes," Fergie breathed in delight. "Quickly."

I gloved up and wrapped her free leg around my waist, and then paused, my dick nudging her entrance, and then waited until Fergie met my gaze, and then pushed inside.

"Sweet Jesus fucking fuck," I groaned, at risk of coming right now.

"Oh god," Fergie moaned. "Move, please."

I pulled out almost the whole way and then slid back inside her, deeper this time. Her leg tightened around me and I thrust harder, finding a rhythm. Her moans became more insistent.

"Yes, like that. Good, again, *again!*"

I held onto the mudguard and picked up my pace. Her head tossed from side to side. I moved between each of her breasts, lapping and sucking, as I pounded into her. Fergie made a string of incoherent noises, her pussy clenching around my dick.

Holy shit, I saw stars. No woman had ever made me see stars, until now.

Skin slapped against skin, the metal of the mudguard shuddering under us.

"If. You. Damage. The. Tractor," she panted with every thrust. "You're. Paying. For. It."

"Time to come, Fergie."

"You can't just order me to orgasm," she hissed as her pussy clenched again.

She was so close. I straightened, maintaining my pace and slipped my hand between us, finding her clit slick and hard.

"That wasn't an order," I grunted, pinching her clit between two fingers. "It was a promise."

One more thrust and Fergie cried out my name over and over, her body trembling.

Electricity sparked down my spine.

I managed to hold on, riding out her orgasm before I slammed into her pussy with a roar, her name echoing off the garage walls.

I slumped forward onto Fergie's chest, my cheek between her tits. The only sound was our heavy breathing, both of us fighting for air. My arm trembled to keep my weight from crushing her.

Slowly, I pushed myself off her and slipped out, both of us moaning again.

Our eyes met. I'd just had sex with Fergie Jones. I smiled, and she smiled back, and it was the most beautiful thing I'd ever seen.

We hadn't talked. We needed to sort things out, but I couldn't talk with my jeans around my ankles and a used condom still on my dick.

I shuffled over to the bin near the counter while Fergie pushed down her skirt, pulled on her tee shirt, and picked up the crankshaft, testing its weight.

I quickly disposed of the condom and pulled up my jeans, and our eyes met again.

"Well, two orgasms for a crankshaft," Fergie laughed. "My lucky day."

I stepped back, feeling like I'd been punched in the gut.

"I didn't come here to swap a part for a quick fuck."

Fergie's face fell.

"I didn't say—"

"That's exactly what you just said."

"But—"

"No buts. No more arguing, Fergie. Aren't you tired of fighting all the time?" She said nothing. "I am, Ferg. I so am."

I swiped my clothes out of the box and my keys off the counter, grasping them with white knuckles.

"Today was never about the parts, or the tractors."

"Wh-what do you mean?"

I loomed over her, briefly glancing at her mouth as she licked her lips.

"Think about it, Fergie. You know exactly what I mean."

I turned on my heel and left by the front door, not looking back.

Fergie

I stared at the side door of Turner's Mechanical in Ballydoon, willing it to open, the smell of smoke in the air. Two days had passed since Dwayne gave me two orgasms and not one word from him since. Not one damn call or email. Nothing.

What the hell did Dwayne mean 'it was never about the parts or the tractors?' It was always about the parts and tractors with us. Tracking down authentic and good quality tractor parts was no easy feat. He loved the thrill of the chase just as much as I did when you found a valuable component in good condition, perfect for your current project.

I rapped again on the door.

I looked down at the Massey Ferguson steering wheel in my hand. I sure as hell was going to tell him what I thought of him having sex with me against the Fordson and then being all obtuse that it 'wasn't about the parts'. Who solved riddles in a post-sex haze?

I jumped as Bruce Turner opened the door.

"Fergie. Wondered when I'd see you," he deadpanned.

"Why?"

He sighed.

"Because of the Great Tractor Feud Between Dwayne and Fergie."

I frowned, looking down at the steering wheel.

Why did we fight? When had that become a thing? It had been a thing since forever.

Aren't you tired of fighting all the time?

"I just came to give this to Dwayne."

I shoved the steering wheel into Bruce's hands. His eyes widened.

"Huh. An original 1956 steering wheel for the Golden Grey." He let out a long whistle. "Pity he can't use it."

"What?" I spat. "Where on earth did he get another one of these at short notice?"

I knew there was no chance Dwayne had found an original steering wheel for his tractor in time for the ag show. I'd set up alerts on all of the sales apps. No steering wheels suitable for his tractors had been listed for sale in the last two days.

"He didn't. Dwayne's been out in the field fighting this bushfire on the national park border."

"Oh." I then realised Bruce wasn't in coveralls. He was dressed in his high vis yellow uniform for the rural fire brigade. "But, when he's back, he can use it."

"Gonna be a long haul out there on the fire front. Said he wouldn't get the tractor finished by the deadline."

"Oh." Since Year Twelve, Dwayne had entered the Vintage Machinery section of the ag show. This would have been his eleventh year. "I heard the fire was bad. How much work does he have left on the Grey?"

"One or two days. He was real close to finishing her. Still needs to run the engine through its checks. But when he's not out in the fire truck with Ryan, he's sleeping in the Ballydoon Hall."

"Oh."

"Why don't you take a look at the Grey while you're here?"

I hesitated.

"I know how much you love your tractors, Fergie."

His lips quirked.

I ducked inside, unable to resist, and immediately saw the F35, the Golden Grey, as they were often called. He'd done a great job with the paintwork, restoring her original colours of light grey on the outside, and the engine in coppery gold. The tyres were a spotless black.

"It's beautiful, honestly. He's done a great job."

"Engine still runs some smoke. Needs maybe five more hours of running time, tops." Bruce shrugged. "But no way he can meet the entry deadline tomorrow with the shifts he's pulling with this damn fire."

Bruce's face was grim.

Panic speared me in my belly.

"Is Dwayne in danger?"

"He'll be okay, love." He held up his hands. "We're all being careful, I promise. Ryan's his team leader and he's the best I've ever seen. Even if I am his proud uncle."

I exhaled with relief and then rolled my lips over my teeth. "Look, Bruce. I've got an idea."

"Go on."

I pitched my thoughts and answered Bruce's questions and finally he agreed, with a handshake.

"Let me make a quick call." I grabbed my mobile from my jeans pocket and dialled. "Hey Dad? It's Fergie. I've got an urgent off-site job and I won't be in for the rest of the day. Tractor business for the ag show."

Dad agreed with a grunt, knowing not to argue with me over tractors.

I hung up and Bruce threw me a set of keys. "Don't let him, or me, down on this one, Fergie."

ᘓᑍᘓ

Dwayne

The front page of the local newspaper declared the Ballydoon Rural Fire Brigade were heroes. A photo of me and our second-in-command, Ryan, all covered in soot and grime took up half of the page.

We'd put the fire out, just in time for the Stanmore District Agriculture Show, and the public holiday for it. And to see Fergie gloat over how she won Grand Champion for her vintage machinery entry.

I should just turn around, go home and sulk—

"Dwayne! You made it!" Bruce strolled over to me, way too cheery.

"Yeah, I'm here."

Not a bloody word from Fergie.

Not that I'd contacted her either. The fire had kept me too busy or exhausted to call her and tell her this wasn't hate, it was—

"What's grinding your gears?"

Fergie. "Nothing. I'm peachy. Just fine."

"You don't look fine." Bruce paused. "This about a girl?"

"No!" I sniffed, looking away.

I couldn't admit to my boss that I'd no idea how I was going to cope if Fergie didn't want me the way I wanted her. And not just sex. I wanted all in.

"Tired from the fire." I faked a yawn.

Bruce rolled his eyes. "Right. Sure."

"I am!" I huffed. "I just wish…" *that I had Fergie in my arms right now.* "That… that the Golden Grey was right here, right now."

"Keep your coveralls on. They moved the display to the main hall this year." Bruce pointed to the entry to the Main Hall. "Does it really matter if the Grey is in here or the Main Hall?"

"Wait… what? I didn't get time to enter her."

"Just go and see, Mr Cranky Pants," he said, ushering me forward.

I shuffled slowly through the doors. The crowd parted in a magic moment, and I saw her: a 1956 F35 Golden Grey Massey Ferguson.

My Grey.

"But I didn't—"

I stumbled forward as Bruce slapped me on the back. "Go on, check her out."

I dumbly made my way through the crowd towards my pride and joy.

I hadn't seen my Grey since the bushfire. How was she even here? I hadn't finished her in time for the ag show and yet, there she was. Shining in the light.

"No way."

My Grey had a steering wheel.

The steering wheel.

I pulled myself up into the seat and ran my fingers around the wheel. It had a dent on the edge like someone had taken a swing at it with an axe and a fleck of green paint on one of the spokes. An all original 1956 Massey Ferguson steering wheel.

The one Fergie had been sitting on for months, refusing to sell to me.

Bruce must have convinced her to sell it to him. For some reason, that made my heart sink. I then noticed the blue ribbon draped over the grille with a golden sash.

I leapt down, huffing a laugh. My Grey had come first in her category and had been judged Best Vintage Machine in the show. Grand Champion.

"Hey, Dwayne."

Fergie was a vision in denim and a tight tee shirt that read 'My favourite ride is a Fergie', with a little graphic of a Massey Ferguson underneath.

Bruce approached us. "Fergie offered to work through the night to attach the wheel and run engine checks. She personally transported the Grey on her own truck to enter it in the comp in time."

I stared at Fergie, open-mouthed.

"This is what they call the grand gesture." Bruce leaned in and whispered. "For goodness' sake, don't screw it up."

He slapped me on the shoulder and left.

"I'm sorry," Fergie blurted, before I could say a word. "I was nervous after we had sex."

A couple of onlookers stared. I growled and they hurried away.

"I panicked. Big time. And I say and do weird things when I

panic. I stole your clothes and ran away, and then I didn't know what to say after we, *you know,* and all I know is mechanics and tractors, so I said that dumb thing about the crankshaft."

I swallowed hard, desperate to hear her next words.

"I get it now, about how it's not about the parts or the tractor. I entered your Grey to say sorry."

It was then that I noticed Fergie's tractor behind her, with a red ribbon for second place stuck on the crankshaft.

A call came over the public speakers asking all vintage farm machinery drivers to attend their vehicles to get ready to move them to the main oval of the showgrounds.

People jumped into action around us.

"Just to say sorry?" I croaked.

"That was part of it. I convinced Bruce to let the enemy finish your Grey in time because I wanted to show you what I felt."

"What do you feel, Fergie?"

"Dwayne, I'm tired of fighting, too." She smiled, hopeful, tentative. "Entering the Grey was the only way I knew how to ask for a chance with you."

I kissed her quickly, ignoring the whistles and cheers around us.

"Break it up, you two! Time to go." A marshal for the Grand Parade waved his clipboard. "This isn't the time for lovey-dovey stuff."

I ignored him, picking up the 'Best Vintage Machinery' sash and draping it over her shoulders.

"You earned this."

"No." Fergie shook her head. "We both did."

"Be mine, Fergie," I whispered.

"Only if you be my Dwayne," she whispered back.

"You've got yourself a deal."

And I kissed her again, taking all the time in the world to show Fergie she was mine.

3
AUTOMATON
FIONA M MARSDEN

I n her heart, Ethne had known he would come. It was her grandfather's funeral and Gert Manning had been Everard Seabrook's favourite protege. He was taller than most of the other mourners, to be expected when you were created to be a superior being. She hadn't known. Not at first. To her, he had been a god. Someone to worship. Instead, he had been a machine.

She shifted her gaze to the minister, sombre in black. He hadn't known Everard, which was probably as well. The old man had been an iconoclast, determined to forge his own path, his own vision for the future. He'd come close to it, using the technology he created to extend his life, long beyond a mere mortal century.

Technology that created beings like Gert Manning to fill the gaps created by three pandemics and another war which was more a trade standoff: leading to the crumbling of formerly great nations, dragging others into the catastrophe. The next pandemic had struck on a world still reeling, unable to draw on the resources which had fought off the previous incursions.

Everard Seabrook had survived it all, promising a Utopian future to those remaining few who could finance his dream. Looking around at the idyllic surrounds of his creation, Ethne had to admit he had kept his promise. There was only one thing he'd failed to do, and that had been his own fault.

"Ethne."

Gert Manning's lush tenor voice didn't sound like a machine. That was the miracle of Everard Seabrook's vision. A machine who was more male than the real thing. Beautiful in his perfection, his pale hair and golden skin a pastiche of the German ideal of centuries past. His eyes should not have been warm, yet they burned with a blue flame she'd only seen in a laboratory. An apt comparison for something made in her grandfather's research facility.

She nodded an acknowledgement. "Hello, Gert. My grandfather would be pleased you came."

"Are you not pleased?"

Indifference. She would try for indifference. "Of course. There are so many of his colleagues here. I wasn't sure if you would tear yourself away from whatever you do these days."

"Research. Always research and development."

"Your choice, or my grandfather's?"

"Both."

Of course. Her grandfather had chosen his successor well. The thought jolted her, turning over her stomach. "Does that mean you'll be coming back?"

His mouth twitched. "Would you prefer I didn't?"

"It has nothing to do with me." Except his return meant she would see him all the time. Like before. Not like before. Now she knew, she was forewarned. You couldn't love a machine. Couldn't want to drag it off to bed and have your way with it six ways till Sunday.

She hadn't known the first time, seeing only his handsome face, his strong lithe body. *His mind.* How could she have thought he was a kindred spirit? The other half of her soul. Machines had no soul.

He shifted to stand beside her as the rest of the mourners filed past. They murmured the conventional words. Death was rare in this world, only coming to those of great age. By then, most people were ready to take the step into the abyss. Would Gert ever be ready?

The other mourners trickled away, leaving them beside the sarcophagus that would be the final resting place of her last relative. Now she was truly alone.

CRXO

Gert hovered, wondering if his presence were a hindrance or a help to Ethne Seabrook at this time. Their parting had been acrimonious. He hadn't expected this cool reserve from her. Hadn't expected her to remember. He suppressed a smile. She was as fiery as her hair suggested, her small frame possessing a large personality. He'd missed her. It had been too many years. More than she knew.

"Are you going inside?"

She glanced around at the formal garden, with its elegant pavilion designed years ago to frame the two marble graves. He remembered when they had been created. One had lain empty for decades, the other containing the remains of Esme Seabrook. Her husband had not been able to save her, the loss of his beloved wife the driver behind his determination and creative urge. All Ethne knew of her parents was that they lay elsewhere. She'd never been given a chance to visit their graves. Her grandfather had been all she needed, and he'd told her not to dwell on the dead.

Ironic, with his own mini-Taj Mahal right outside his back door.

She shifted, looking up at him with vivid green eyes, glossy with unshed tears. "Yes. Take me inside. I don't want to be here."

He wrapped his arm around her shoulders to guide her from the gardens and the presence of death. She was warm under his touch, the heat of her seeping into his skin, the sensation raising the hairs on his forearm. A wash of pleasure lit up his synapses. It had been far too long.

Inside the building, as spartan inside as the outside had been lovely, Ethne shook him off and led the way to the common living area. "How long are you here for? Where will you be staying?"

She spun around at his silence. "Aren't you going to answer me?"

"I'll be living here, in this house. Permanently, at your grandfather's insistence."

"No. I won't have it. You'll have to find somewhere else."

"You have no authority over me, Ethne."

"But this is my home."

There was a lost, bewildered air about her. He wanted to comfort her; hold her in his arms and soothe the emptiness she felt at the loss of family. The loneliness he could understand too well.

He wanted her too. Had always wanted her. He'd known Ethne Seabrook was his from the first time he'd met her, introduced by her grandfather. Far too young and naive. It had taken years for her to grow up. Maybe the death of her grandfather would be the final push she needed.

"It might be your home, but it is also the home of the head of the Foundation. At this time, that role belongs to me."

"You're not even human. How could they choose you?"

"Intelligence and knowledge are not the sole province of human beings. Thanks to Everard Seabrook, there are other beings who can bring many of those qualities to the table."

She folded her arms across her perfectly formed breasts, drawing his unwilling attention. "I don't want to live with you."

"Seabrook House has enough rooms, spread over enough area that you need never see me."

"I suppose you'll be in Grandfather's rooms."

"They are the most convenient for the person in charge of the Foundation."

"I'll move my things."

"It hardly seems worth it. It's not like you actually lived in your grandfather's suite."

"It's next door; far too close."

He moved away, heading for the kitchen. "I'm hungry and thirsty. Is there anything to eat?"

She trailed after him. "You could have gone to the reception for the Foundation members. There would have been plenty of food."

He pulled out a bottle of purified water and a dish of salad. His instructions had been clear, and someone had carried them out. An excellent start. He chose a stool at the end of the bench and opened the bottled water.

She raised her brows. "Why do you need food anyway? Can't you simply plug yourself into a power outlet?"

"I don't like the taste. Too much zap and not enough zest."

She perched on one of the other stools, leaving a gap between them. "Could you, if you needed to eat and there wasn't any food?"

"Perhaps. Though my biological symbiosis requires some direct nourishment."

"It doesn't sound very practical."

"Your grandfather wasn't interested in being practical. He was saving humanity."

"By creating synthetic humans." She snorted. "It wouldn't work. Robots could never be as good as humans."

"We prefer the term automaton. However, you can call me Gert. I am a person; however differently you may view my creation."

"You're different, aren't you, from the usual robots. They aren't organic, and while they're clever enough for their tasks, they can't usually compete intellectually with humans."

"Your grandfather was experimenting with a whole range of options. Some became useful, others remain as ideas that never quite made it past the concept stage."

"Will you carry them out?"

He nodded, eyeing the food on his fork. "If it seems viable."

"I'm really stuck with you, aren't I?"

"Consider it an opportunity."

She rested her chin on her hand, her elbow propped on the bench. "An opportunity for what?"

"To get to know me all over again. This time you might like me."

"I did like you, until I found out it wasn't real."

Shoving the food away, he spun around on the stool. "What part wasn't real? The talking all night. The time spent simply getting to know each other while we ate or explored the natural world. Making love until we were exhausted. What part of that wasn't real?"

"You weren't real. And you were never exhausted."

He smiled at that memory, albeit unwillingly. Gert couldn't remember the last time he'd had cause to smile. "Are you complaining, my love?"

"Of course not. I meant— Oh, you know what I meant. And don't use endearments you don't mean."

"I know what you mean. I know what I mean too. I meant every word, every endearment."

"You can't. Machines don't know about love. Not really. They can't." She slid from the stool. "I'm going to my room. You can make yourself at home." She waved randomly at her surroundings, "I'm sure you will."

Ethne flung herself on the bed in her room and scrunched her eyes shut. *She would not cry.* Not over an oversized hunk of machinery who'd been made in the image of every woman's dream. It wasn't fair. Her whole body prickled with awareness of him. She should be able to control her hormones, shouldn't she? It was her grandfather's fault. He'd plucked Gert Manning's specs out of her dreams. Of course, she'd reacted to him.

For all her talk, and his snarky backchat, they weren't going to be able to avoid each other. She had her own responsibilities at the Foundation. She'd met with her grandfather every day to report on the children's program.

It was her choice to oversee the home placements for the young children who arrived daily at the Foundation school. Her longing for a family could be sublimated by contact with the children, who often had no parents of their own. With her own experience of loss, she found solace helping others who had no memory of loving parents.

Unless Gert had his own ideas about her responsibilities. She had her grandfather to thank for allowing her to follow her natural inclination. As the new director, Gert could do a clean sweep, putting in his own preferred subordinates. She couldn't let that happen.

Flinging herself into the shower room, she flinched at the bleary-eyed woman facing her. She couldn't meet him like this. It wasn't only her pride at stake. She had something to prove, after her immature reception of his invasion of her life and home.

Showered and dressed in something clingy and short, Ethne re-evaluated her appearance. She wasn't going for sexy. It's not like she wanted to resume that part of their old relationship. All the same, it didn't hurt to remind him of what he'd thrown away. She shook her head, confused at the way her thoughts were running. Vague and disjointed. She'd rejected him, not the other way round. She'd found out Gert Manning was part of a top-secret project her grandfather had kept private even from his closest colleagues and his family. He should have told her. Trusted her.

It would have made it easier if she'd been warned. Though armed with the knowledge, bracing herself to face her former lover still didn't seem easy.

She hesitated at the door that had always led from her rooms to her grandfather's apartment. It had been a place of comfort, where she was secure in the knowledge of her grandfather's love. Now it contained Gert Manning, the source of her pain. It shouldn't hurt after all this time. Anger helped. Anger would take her through this confrontation. She had to hold onto the anger so the other feelings wouldn't take over. The wanting. The need.

Pushing the door open, she launched herself into the living area of the suite. *He must listen.*

The room was empty.

Ethne turned slowly, taking in the space. It was the same as in her grandfather's time. Nothing had been changed. The same books. The same photographs. The one of her taken recently sat in pride of place on the shelf under the flatscreen on the wall. There were a couple of others, taken with her grandfather, all fairly current. None of her as a child. It had never struck her before.

"Ethne? What do you want?"

"What makes you think I want something?" Although the question became moot when her gaze absorbed the expanse of bare chest above the low-slung towel wrapped around his narrow hips. She was such a cliche, drooling over physical assets when it was what was inside that counted.

"I'm guessing you've remembered you're an employee of the Foundation, and as such, answer to me for your position."

"Are you going to change things?"

He walked toward her, and she resisted the temptation to back away. There was moisture in his hair and on his bare chest, a drop or two in the fine, almost invisible fuzz.

"Only where I think it necessary."

She could smell the fresh washed scent of him. He shouldn't smell so good. She was hungry for him and if the profile of his towel were an indication, he wasn't indifferent.

"Like what you see?"

A flick of his long, elegant fingers sent the towel tumbling to the floor. *Oh yes. I like very much.*

She forced her eyes to focus on his face. "I think I should go now that I have your reassurances."

"You could stay and have a drink with me. To make me feel welcome."

"I don't think it's a good idea."

His hand stroked a long path from her jawline to the low-cut neckline of her dress. "Did you wear this for me?"

"Of course not." She stepped backwards, and he reached past her, nudging the door shut.

The hard timber marked the farthest distance she could go. To open it, she had to brush past Gert. Already one of his arms formed a barrier and as she hesitated, he planted his free hand flat on the other side.

"Tell me you want to leave."

"I want to leave."

"Not like a little girl in a temper. Make me believe it."

Her heart thumped against her ribcage. There must be magnets in his body creating a tug she found hard to resist. Her throat was raw from swallowed emotions. "I don't want to go." It came out in a whisper, but, this close, he couldn't fail to hear.

"Stay then."

Slow, achingly slow, he brought his body against hers, pressing her against the cool surface of the door, her hands clenched at her sides. She wanted to touch.

It was all on her. Unfisting her hands, she smoothed them over the bony protuberances of his pelvis. His stomach flexed under her thumbs, and she widened her grasp, brushing along the line of muscle that led to the hard ridge pressed against her belly. The flesh quivered under her touch. He shuddered, as if the strain of holding himself still was immense.

She couldn't stay silent. She needed him to act. "Touch me. I want you to touch me."

His body softened under her hands and then tautened as he stroked down her sides and up again, under her skirt.

He pulled her lacy thong down, dropping it to her ankles. She kicked it off, along with the low-heeled sandals.

He lifted her and she wrapped her legs around his thighs, crossing her ankles to steady them for what was coming. Long fingers probed between her thighs and a grunt of satisfaction told her he'd found her wet and ready.

There were no preliminaries. God knew, she'd been primed and eager before she'd walked through this door. His thrust lifted her, jamming her hard against the timber. He stilled as if he found the same magic she had sought in the moment. So long between, so much need. So much pain.

He shifted, bracing his legs. She clung to him, arms wrapped over his shoulders, fingers tangled in his hair. The second thrust was feeling his way. So good, so much. Her insides crackled with heat and fire, liquid flame lighting the darkness of years of emptiness.

The rhythm started at a slow, even pace, matching the rhythm of her heart; physically linked together, blood flowing through the connection between to keep them synchronised. He followed the beat as it picked up pace. *Too much too soon.* Her muscles tightened in flux around him and his thrusts became uneven as she fled reality to some unknown dimension where only she and he remained, beings of light and sensation. No hurt, no pain. Only them as they were meant to be.

A groan from Gert echoed her own cries and there was a satisfaction barely acknowledged that he, too, was in flight, unanchored to this world – this actuality that had torn them apart. Here there were no barriers, no expectations. Only love.

Love?

Ethne blinked back into sanity.

How did he do this to her? Make her forget.

He lowered her to the floor, steadying her with his large hands on her waist. His expression was wary, brows tilted toward the small crease at the bridge of his nose. "Are you all right?"

She adjusted her dress, looking around for the scrap of underwear. "I'm all right. It's not like I haven't had sex before." Though maybe not against her grandfather's door.

"I'm sorry. I was careless."

She looked at him for the first time since they'd uncoupled. He looked tired, holding the towel loosely over his penis. He was never tired. "Careless? It's not like you can make me pregnant."

"I'm not one of the automatons at the recreation centre."

"Aren't you?" Trying to put disdain into her splintered self was harder than it should be. She'd only succeeded in looking petty and childish.

CRWO

Ethne looked shattered. Gert pulled in a breath, taking it deep. He had to keep calm.

"I didn't mean it to happen. Not like that." Like an animal in heat.

"How did you mean it to happen?"

He laughed, more at himself than at the situation. "Foolishly, I planned to court you, as I'd done before. Dinner perhaps. Picnics in the park."

"I'm not hungry."

There was something in the way she looked at him.

Something different. *She* was different. A woman's knowledge shone from her eyes. Perhaps her grandfather had been right. She'd struggled with the challenges of the reality she was only starting to discover. There was more to come, but now she had the strength to face the truth.

"What do you want?"

"I want to make love to you, the way we did in my memories."

He nodded, his mouth too dry to formulate the words.

Her hand reached for his. "In my room. It was always in my room."

Her bedroom was the same, soft shades of ocean green that matched her everchanging eyes. She stripped her clothes off with a haste that did his self-esteem good. The vision of her naked body did other things to him, bringing him to full strength.

For him it was a visit to an enchantment he'd long thought lost as she explored his body with mouth and tongue and gentle fingers. When she straddled him, he was more than ready, the ache in his gut only half the intensity of the pressure in his chest as his heart pumped out its joy.

The way she lowered herself onto his shaft was a lesson in torture soon overtaken by pleasure as she rode him, leaning forward to take his mouth, owning it with her tongue and teeth. She took him to heaven and back, even if it were a place an automaton couldn't aspire to.

When it was over and they lay content, he knew it was time to be honest. Later when the loving was done.

Gert was serious now, the relaxed man after their coming together gone as they'd crossed the forecourt of the Foundation's property.

"Your grandfather didn't want you to know this, but he's gone, and I think you need to know. Otherwise, you'll never come to terms with the world you live in."

"Is this about my job?"

He paused at the door of the massive storage facility she'd never had cause to enter. "It's about all the children."

Goosebumps peppered her skin as they travelled the long white corridor into the heart of the facility. Cold dread sat in her gut. "It looks more like a hospital than a warehouse."

"You aren't far wrong, yet it does function as a type of storage."

The passage appeared endless, but Gert halted a few hundred metres along, at a blank door, hardly noticeable in the expanse of pristine white.

The murmur of voices hit her first and faces turned at their entrance. Gert nodded and they went back to their instruments. She suspected some were microscopes, but others she didn't recognise. "What are they doing?"

"Gene analysis. The genetic materials are thoroughly checked before use."

"Genetic engineering?"

"To a point. They scan for debilitating diseases. Genetic anomalies that have no adverse effects are kept in the interests of a diverse population."

"Are they all going to turn out to be superior beings."

His mouth curved up at one corner. "I'm an experimental model. Not to be repeated."

"Seriously, are there others like you?"

One of the nearby scientists looked up and exchanged an odd look with Gert before returning to his work. Ethne glanced around at the others, but they were all focussing on their individual tasks.

He exited the room through a side door into another featureless corridor. "In my father's house are many mansions." **

"And many corridors. How do people find their way? It's like a maze."

"We're generally smarter than rats in this facility. It helps save time."

The tour went through a series of laboratories and rooms. He showed her the cryogenic chambers where the genetic material was stored. "Surely you don't need this giant facility to assist in reproductive therapies."

"It's not exactly reproductive therapies. Not of the kind you mean."

He opened a door and she stood frozen at the sight of rows and rows of cylinders. Floating in each cylinder were embryos in various stages of development.

"Cloning?" She shoved at him, but he didn't move. "You're doing cloning? Isn't that against a Convention?"

"That world is gone, Ethne. It's only in the history books your grandfather wanted you to read. We live in a pod, isolated from a world that will take generations to heal from the devastation human beings wreaked upon it."

"Is it just us, here?"

"There are others, scattered around the world. Your grandfather was able to rally enough interest to put plans in place for this eventuality."

"What about the rest of the world?"

"They saved everyone they could, but that generation is all gone to dust. More time has passed than you realise."

"The people here are descendants of those survivors."

He indicated the embryos. "These are the descendants. A combination of contaminants and viruses left most infertile."

"It's taken this long to get the technology up to standard?"

"The Foundation was working against time. The first generation of automatons were basic utility machines. To build and provide services. When they realised there would be no children to replace the survivors, your grandfather began creating cyborgs. It worked in with using technology to lengthen lives, keeping them strong. He gave the cyborgs synaptic brains, so they could learn and retain memories."

Ethne leaned against the wall, her legs trembling jellies under the bombardment of so much information. "Where do you fit in?"

"A special project. Your grandfather knew he couldn't live forever, even with all the technological advances at his command. He was already an old man when this began. He doubted if his mind would cope with a transfer into a new synaptic capsule and he wasn't prepared to take the risk."

She sucked in a breath. It began to make sense, her confusion giving way to understanding. "Leaders. He wanted leaders. Someone to take command. Yet you're part human. Why would he do that?"

"The aim was to create a transitional generation, until the human population has time to fulfil its destiny."

"How many? Of the people I know, how many are not fully human?"

"You should be asking the other question."

"No. I can't." She plunged across the room to confront the sleeping face of a child close to the end of its gestation period. "I can't."

"The children, Ethne. None of the adults are capable of reproducing. Your grandfather hadn't completed his experiments on the next generation of automatons. There were issues he hadn't expected." He stroked the cylinder with a gentle hand. "These children will be able to reproduce. They will grow up in families of automatons, maybe they will fall in love, create partnerships, have families of their own. Fully human."

"Doesn't it worry you, becoming redundant?"

"Isn't that the nature of humanity? One generation following the next. Dying in due time, knowing the children and grandchildren will go on. Hopefully doing better than they did in stewardship of this world."

"I don't understand you. When you talk this way, you sound human. Like Grandfather."

"He was the defining influence in my life, my creation. He was my creator. My god, if you will."

"I suppose it helped him, having lost his wife and child, to be able to create life."

Gert was silent, leaning his forehead against the cylinder. It was an odd dichotomy, the part human robot, seeming reflected in the glass by something he'd never been. Had Gert arrived fully formed in this human guise? No womb to nurture, no childhood. Only adulthood and responsibility. Not like her, filled with memories of a childhood of laughter though it contained no remembered parental figures. She hunched her shoulders against the tightness in her chest.

Did she even have a heart? But at least she understood now. With understanding came pain, yet there was a kind of relief as well.

She moved closer, resting her hand beside his, her pinky brushing against his fingers, seeking the faintest touch. "Where do my memories come from?"

His sigh shuddered through his body. "They were Esme's. From a world long gone."

"They meddled with them, didn't they, so I couldn't see the background detail, the people? I suppose that's where my DNA came from."

Gert took her in his arms. "You aren't a clone. You're an automaton. Yes, your DNA came from Esme, to create those parts of you that are human. Your mind is not human, only your memories."

"I was the failed experiment?" Her questionable heart tightened in her chest. She pressed hard against Gert to ease the pain. His exhalation as he spoke warmed her skin.

"Not you. Your predecessor. Your grandfather realised at the last that one of the things that trigger emotional growth was adversity. Your life had been too perfect. Each test subject wiped clean of memories to start fresh."

"But I remember you. How can I remember you if I was a different person?"

"Your grandfather kept those memories. This time he gave them back to you."

Relief fought with anger. "Why would he do that? Why would he deliberately hurt me? He could have taken that all away."

"Is that what you want to happen... what you wish for? To forget about us?"

Ethne buried her face in his shoulder, imbibing his scent. With it came memories, so many memories. Falling in love, Gert's old-fashioned courting under the benevolent eye of her grandfather. Making love. Her skin tingled as warmth flowed through her, igniting where her body touched his. "No, I don't want to forget. I want all the memories, both wonderful and painful. I want you. I love you."

His mouth brushed hers in a benediction. "Thank you. I have waited a long time to hear those words again, my love."

"How long?"

He pulled back, keeping his arms loosely around her, studying her face. "Decades."

She tightened her hold on him. "Your adversity. I'm sorry."

"You are worth the wait."

She caught sight of the child beyond them, sleeping and sucking its thumb. "Will we be able to adopt children?"

"If you wish. There are other options for us."

Ethne pressed a hand to her stomach. "Grandfather made it possible? For both of us?"

"Esme's DNA in you. His DNA in me. We are capable in all ways to produce their genetic children. Our children."

"Why didn't it happen before?"

"He wanted maturity in both. I complied with his directive to wait."

"I love you so much. Thank you for waiting." She reached up to kiss his beautiful mouth and he leaned into it, absorbing her into him.

The kiss was all it was meant to be, deep with emotion and pent-up desire. He pulled back with a laugh. "I think it's time to go."

Still throbbing with the sensations he always brought to life, she stared up at him. "Why?"

He brought his mouth to her ear. "Not in front of the children, dear."

Her startled laughter sparked a gleam in his eyes.

His placed his hand against her palm and wrapped his fingers around hers.

"Time to live and love and laugh, together."

She snuggled closer as they walked down the long corridor. Together. "Especially love."

Notes:

** Here the character quotes John 14:2 from the King James Bible, in the Public Domain

https://www.gutenberg.org/files/10/10-h/10-h.htm#The_Gospel_According_to_Saint_John

4
TWO MONTHS, FOUR DAYS
GEORGIA MOORE

Day 1

R iley dumps a canvas bag in the ship's cargo hold. The *thunk* of it on the metal floor is echoed by the surge of relief in my gut.

"Thanks for coming," he says. "I wasn't sure you would."

"Neither was I."

He looks haggard. His shirt bags where it used to pull across his chest. His dark hair is longer, his face unshaven, brown eyes without the warmth that always made my chest light.

My chest isn't light now. It's heavy with a heart that's been iced over for two months. Two months to the day that Riley left me on Jilyria without a note or a goodbye. No hint he was even alive until a few hours ago.

I hear my siblings' voices in my head, telling me I don't need to go through with this, but running my gaze over Riley, seeing he's alive and whole, eases something in me that's been tightening for months. Taking a steadying breath, I shut the exterior door and the voices in my head disappear.

Riley's gaze slides over my hair, my neck, shoulders, chest. My hands. Relief is palpable in his shaky exhale.

The unfrozen centre of my heart warms and he's done nothing but stand there. I haven't even gotten an apology.

Instead of demanding one, my bleeding heart asks, "Do you need a medbay visit?"

Riley's attention returns to my face. "I need an immuno-booster and some anti-scar gel. Could do with a vitamin injection too."

"You know where it is. I'll get us moving."

I leave him in the cargo hold, hollowness growing in my chest with every step away. How could he have left me for two entire months? My legs shake with the need to turn around, throw my arms around him and feel his body against mine, smell the vanilla and spice of his musk, kiss him until I can't breathe. Until I forget the past two months of worry.

But absence can only make a heart grow fonder for so long before the balance tips.

I stare at the kaleidoscope of colours outside the ship as we jump through space, body heavy in the Captain's chair. Riley's onboard and I feel... confused. I've pictured our reunion dozens, if not hundreds, of times. They ran the gamut from weeping with joy to violent arguments to naked celebration.

Instead, I got nothing. Banked emotions waiting for that spark of lightning to set off a storm. Riley used to tease me about bottling things up. He called my emotional explosions 'Taylor-nados' and himself my storm catcher.

As we drop out of our first jump, messages run across my Captain's panel from my parents, brother, and eldest sister.

Are you on your way back? Should we come over tonight?

I've got a new laser-pistol. Do I need to inflict damage to the douche?

Are you with Riley? Are you okay? How are you feeling?

I watch the messages until they time out and disappear. I have no clear answer to any of them. How *am* I feeling? I close my eyes and dig into the storm inside me, finding crystallised relief, hot anger, aching desire, stinging rejection. And over it all, like a layer of misting rain, fondness. Even trapped inside ice, my heart beats hard for Riley.

Sighing, I message my sister.

I'm fine. We're halfway back. Let the others know. See you soon.

The sound of Riley's footsteps reaches the bridge. My shoulders bunch. He'd strapped himself into a chair in medbay for the first jump. I should've expected he'd come to me before the next.

He's hovering when I look over my shoulder, his arms loose by his sides but tension at his eyes.

"Can I join you?" he asks.

I swallow around a dry throat. "Sure."

He takes the chair beside mine. "You upgraded the control panels," he comments, looking around. "And the lights in the rest of the ship."

"Better efficiency."

He hums and nods, then runs his broad palms up and down his thighs. He's thinking hard on something, so I take the time to look at him. Aside from the obvious neglected grooming, I can't find a thing wrong. On my next exhale, a heaviness lifts from my shoulders.

Riley's hands pause atop his knees and he turns to me. "Taylor. I need to tell you why I left."

My breath catches in my throat like a clenched fist.

"No apology?"

"My apology won't mean anything without the explanation."

Always so measured and logical. Is that why his abrupt departure hit me so hard? There were no signs of him planning it, or even considering it.

We're pulled into another jump and the ship vibrates like a luvia palm in a hurricane. It's enough to rattle my insides.

Riley glances around the bridge as the vibration continues.

"Another new addition?"

"No." I lean over the controls. Our jump path is steady and a basic diagnostic scan shows nothing, but the turbulence continues.

"Anything?" Riley asks.

"Nothing showing. But I don't—"

The shaking worsens enough that I grab for the secondary harness and strap it over my chest. Riley does the same.

"When was the last time you got your jump circuit serviced?" he asks.

I run a secondary diagnostic of the engine systems as we're dragged through the jump path. I can't drop us out unless I want to risk tearing my ship into pieces.

"Taylor," Riley prompts, an edge to his voice.

"Five months."

"*Taylor.* They're meant to be done every three. The pressure placed on those nodes—"

"You think I don't know that?" My bones rattle against each other. I'm shaking so much it's hard to press the buttons on the control panel.

"You fixed the lights but not the jump circuit?"

A metallic groaning builds, echoing through the ship.

"I've been doing my own services. Waiting for the mock-9 system to be publicly available."

"This machine is a barrel of spare parts," he growls, "and your skill only takes them so far."

"Hey!" Raised voice. Taylor-nado is here.

"I told you countless times you need to upgrade."

"I *have* been upgrading."

A louder groan, then a metallic *clang*.

There's sudden pressure. Weight crushing my organs and stealing my breath. One second. Two. Three. Four. Five. The stabilisers finally correct and I suck in lungfuls of air.

Riley gasps, wasting no time before saying, "I don't mean parts. I mean the entire thing. You're only delaying the inevitable."

"This *barrel of spare parts* is my life."

"No. *You* are your life and you're worth more than second-hand parts and constant repairs. Buy a gods-damn new ship."

"Don't tell me what to do! You lost that right when you left me."

Quiet descends like a slap. Sudden and sharp.

It's not just our words that have stopped, the ship has gone quiet too, only the barest vibration from the engine, over which I hear my own shallow breathing and Riley's uneven inhales and exhales. Outside the window is calm black and pinpricks of stars. No planet in sight.

"Taylor." The word cracks at the end.

I turn back to Riley. His eyes are wide, more terrified now than during the ship's ordeal.

My organs ache like they've been scraped against sandstone. I should be checking the ship, but instead I say, "It's been two months. *Two months.*"

There's pain in his eyes. "I am so deeply sorry."

The words are what I want, but the satisfaction is hollow. He's right. I need the why.

C8&0

The engine room offers no answers to why we were thrown from the jump path. I check everything twice, and only find a new problem.

"The power cells are majorly depleted," I tell Riley, re-entering the bridge.

"Okay. It's only one more jump. The back-up cell should cover it."

"It would, but the jump circuit's blown. We can't relink." I drop into the Captain's chair and stare out at the star-studded blackness. "It's nine days to Jilyria. The power cells won't stretch that far unless I power down everywhere but the bridge and Captain's quarters, and narrow the parameters on the life support system."

"Ah." Riley rubs a palm over his unshaven jaw. "But we can make it?"

"Yes."

"What about water? Food?"

"Not an issue."

"Alright."

In the silence, my thoughts race as I face down nine days in confined quarters with Riley. Shit. I'm not — I can't — I *need* to fix the ship.

"Hey." He leans across to me and I get a hint of his vanilla scent. "I know this isn't ideal, but since we're stuck—"

"Stop." I stand so abruptly my vision swims. "I'm sorry but I can't deal with... *more* today."

Riley falls silent but I feel his gaze on me as I recross my arms and hold still until my vision clears. I need to hear his explanation. I *want* to hear it. But I'm not in the headspace to listen objectively and I owe it to us to wait until I am.

"I'm going to move supplies from the mess into the kitchenette in my quarters," I say eventually.

"Wait." Riley stands, shifting into my path. His hands clench and unclench at his sides. "You'll hear me out eventually?"

There's negligible space between us and the proximity lights a match beneath my frosty heart, pumping blood thick through my veins as I breathe him in.

I want Riley still.

I want him to wrap me in his strong arms and kiss me until everything feels better, until my insides stop scraping against each other and all I feel is pleasure. But desire has never been our issue and while Riley's physically closer than he's been in months, he's still as far away from me.

Day 2

Riley steps into the dining nook and my stomach swoops. He's showered and shaved. He looks like the man I saw at the markets on Hinali all those years ago. I'd followed him for an hour because he was so damn gorgeous I couldn't take my eyes off him. Short brown hair, dark skin, broad shoulders, muscles noticeable even when relaxed, and a perfect full mouth in the centre of a square jaw. It was the mouth that gut-punched me that day, when I saw it curl into a grin as he chatted with a vendor selling second-hand audio tech.

He'd noticed me eventually, had walked over and introduced himself. We spent the day absorbed in each other before I had to catch the last shuttle back to the university where I taught. We'd exchanged comm-codes and he promised to message the next day. And he did.

Stomach still hovering like it's filled with helium, I watch him prepare food with ease. I haven't upgraded anything here since our week-long trip to the Frida Nebula.

His body tenses when he faces the table. I push the chair on my left out and he sits. A few months ago, he would have pressed a kiss to my temple on the way down or pulled me onto his lap.

My stomach churns. I'm sick of the distance between us. "I'm ready to hear it. Your explanation. Why did you leave?"

He faces me. "To try and find Ethan."

Everything in me stiffens. "Your brother?"

His food remains untouched. "I got a time-sensitive lead and I followed it. Had to buy passage on a supply ship."

"And?"

"Nothing." Riley exhales roughly, eyes pinched. "I don't know if the information was dodgy, or he was never there."

A sensation like a clenched fist in my throat makes it hurt to swallow. "Why didn't you take me with you?"

"Xen-Lian's only just been brought into the Alliance," he hedges. "There's a lot of unrest."

I swallow bitter air. "You could have at least told me."

His gaze slides off my face momentarily. "You'd have wanted to come along."

"And?" My eyebrows lift. "We were engaged, Riley. That's the whole point. We're meant to be a team. *Through triumph and trials,*" I say the words we should have shared at our bonding ceremony.

"*Are* engaged," is the only comment Riley makes.

His gaze drops to my bare ring finger. He must have noticed already, but this is the first time he's drawing attention to it.

I move the hand onto my lap.

"You're angry," Riley says.

"I thought you'd left me."

"Taylor." My name bursts from his chest and he grabs my left hand, touching me for the first time since our reunion. Heat burns through me so fast it steals my breath. My body cants toward his until we're breathing the same air.

"You're the love of my life. I'll never leave you."

The words sink into my bones. Gods, his blunt adoration still makes my heart race, my muscles tremble.

My bed is *right there.*

"But you did." I stand and pull my hand away. "And you didn't contact me — let me know you were *alive* — for two entire months."

His eyebrows draw together. "I tried. They aren't connected to the satellite network yet."

"What about paper messages? There weren't any courier ships leaving?"

"No." He jerks from his seat and goes for his bag, rummaging around before unearthing a bundle of papers. He throws them and they skid across the table, my hand reflexively stopping them from sliding completely off.

I glance down and my breath catches. My fingers trace over handwritten letters. My name.

"I contacted you the second I could." His voice scrapes out raw and I believe him.

He walks slowly to me, a desperate edge to his voice. "It wasn't meant to take so long. I thought it'd be a couple of days and I'd be able to contact you the entire time. I had visions of video-calling and introducing my brother to my fiancée. Bringing him to our home and having him stand beside me at our ceremony."

The fantasy digs like claws in my skin because that dream of reuniting with Ethan had become mine, too. *Ours*. But he didn't give me the chance to chase it with him.

I lift my hand off the letters and step back. "You left me behind." The words catch in my throat.

"Taylor." Riley's forehead furrows. He takes my hand again, unfurling the digits. "How do I fix it? How do we get back to where we were?"

Tingles run up my arm. The desire to take him to bed and let him fix us that way pulls at my gut, but I can't do to us what he's accused me of doing to my ship. Repairing faults with temporary fixes without addressing the heart of the issue.

I don't trust he'll take me with him next time.

ᚷᚱᛒᛃ

The day is long and with so little of the ship available, I spend a lot of time in Riley's company. Awareness of him sits like a blanket on my shoulders. Every tiny touch sends goosebumps along my skin and starts a warmth low in my belly that doesn't fade.

Our video comms were damaged, but thankfully I can still send and receive messages, and spend most of the day doing so, attempting to distract myself from vacillating between wanting to read Riley's letters and pretending they don't exist.

Riley tries to engage me in conversation, offering more explanations and apologies. I snap after lunch, tell him point blank I need time to digest what he said at breakfast. He backs off then, but even out of sight he's constantly in my thoughts.

I go to bed early, but sleep doesn't come. It's obviously the same for Riley.

"Get in here," I snap after his eighth groan of the evening. I don't know if he's playing me, or if the futon really is that uncomfortable for his six-foot frame.

We lie on opposite edges of the bed, facing away from each other. I shove my hands beneath my armpits and burrow my face into my pillow so I'm not tempted to roll over, cling to his body and drag my nose up his bare chest to fill my lungs with his vanilla and spice scent.

CR&O   CR&O

Day 3

My body is warm all over, my back pressed against a solid chest. It's been a while since I've dreamed like this. Knuckles slowly rub across my belly where my singlet has rucked up, right at the edge of my shorts, and heat blooms up to my breasts and down to my core. I rub my thighs together and press myself back against a growing hardness.

A deep male groan sounds, and a kiss is pressed to the back of my neck. My nipples harden and I rock my hips back, rewarded with more kisses. The hand slides beneath the front of my shorts, and my leg lifts over a solid thigh, giving them room to cup me and press down. I sigh when a finger slips into my wetness and drags up, sliding gently over my clit, turning my limbs heavy.

The finger flicks and I gasp, the jolt of pleasure-pain breaking through my sleep-fog.

Not a dream.

I bolt upright, yanking the hand away, and spin to kneel beside Riley. His hand drops from my grip and lands on my bare thigh.

Riley's attention is fixed on my face, his pupils blown wide. Our gazes hold for endless moments. Can he tell how torn I am between staying and running away?

Eyes still on mine, he inches his hand up my goosebump-covered thigh. I watch it reach the hem of my shorts then pause. I'm trembling. My breath comes in short, snatched gasps. I want him, this, so much my insides are already clenching around nothing.

When I don't move, his hand slides beneath the fabric.

"*Taylor,*" he breathes my name like a benediction and I shiver.

"I— I can't." The words are croaky, barely audible, but he pulls away immediately.

I walk unsteadily into the tiny bathroom, then strip and step inside the shower cubicle. I'm so wet it's coating my upper thighs.

I slam the cleaning cycle button and the cold pressurised water shocks me enough to help me claw back some control. I still throb for him, but I can rise above that because we can't get through this with sex, tempting as it is. His explanations and apologies mean something, they do, but they're not everything.

Because how can they reassure me he won't leave me behind again?

CЗВО   CЗВО

Day 4

Another day spent orbiting each other, another night we start apart and by morning have collided. The cold shower is less effective, and when I step out wrapped in a towel, it's like I've been sucker-punched.

Riley sits on my bed in his black briefs, nursing a bundle of white fabric. The dress he helped me select for our bonding ceremony.

I clear my throat and his head snaps up. His eyes are glassy with unshed tears, but I see hope there, too. His fingers don't stop moving over the scalloped edges and tiny buttons. "You kept the dress."

Three times I tried throwing it away. My heart ached each attempt. The third sent me into a panic attack and without Riley to ground me, it took an age to come out of. I counted every button on that thing. In dreams, I've imagined Riley slowly undoing all of them.

He returns the dress carefully to the clothes chest before facing me. "We need to talk."

"About Ethan?"

He shakes his head. "I think we can fix the jump circuit."

My mouth pops open. "What? How?"

"You narrowed the life support parameters," Riley tells me unnecessarily. "There's an energy cube going unused."

I frown.

"Why would — You want to do a hard reset." My pulse accelerates. "Patch the cube to the jump circuit, then run it at full capacity. It'll act like an organic part."

He nods, taking a single step closer. "The closest hinge-point is an hour away. We can re-join the jump path and be home in less than two hours."

Why didn't I think of that?

The answer comes immediately.

"That requires a spacewalk." You shouldn't do that alone — someone's got to be monitoring from inside the ship — and because I haven't been seeing Riley and me as a team, it didn't occur to me.

"Yes," Riley confirms. "I could have done it alone but—"

"You *what*?" Pressure builds in my chest.

"—but I wanted to talk to you about it first because you're right, Taylor." His features are tight, an apology in his eyes. "We're a team."

More harsh words threaten to burst out of me, but I take a slow breath. He contemplated the solo spacewalk but didn't go through with it. He's shared his thoughts with me so we could make the decision together. My lungs loosen.

He takes two more steps and I need to tilt my head to look into his eyes. My right hand fists around the knot in my towel as a fiery awareness of how little clothing there is between us rushes around my chest.

His gaze holds mine, steady and earnest. "We face challenges together."

"What about with Ethan?" I ask, addressing head on the decision that brought us here.

"Next time I get a lead, I'm telling you straight away." He inches closer. I feel the heat from his chest on my knuckles. "We'll make a plan together."

"Do you swear it?"

He goes silent. He never lies and he never breaks his promises, not a single one since his first promise to message me the day we met.

My heart thuds as I watch his face. He reaches slowly for my left hand, picks it up and cradles it, sliding a thumb over the ring finger. Heat moves up my arm and pierces my heart, speeding my pulse so the fire in my chest spreads throughout my body. My next breath is shaky.

"Taylor." His gaze holds mine, expression open, showing all his hope, all his love, his commitment. Desire, too. "I promise."

I thought the tension had left me when I first saw Riley was okay, but now it's like he's cut a suspension cord with his words. Apology. Explanation. Promise. My chest lifts as I gasp, warmth spiralling through my torso.

It's me who moves.

I grab his shoulders and wrap my legs around his hips. His hands slot below my thighs with the ease of muscle memory.

We're already kissing as we manoeuvre, Riley shifting me higher, hands moving to my ass, me angling his head until our lips align perfectly. Two months apart is nothing against six years of connection.

As we kiss, his heat lances through me at every contact point. Lips, hands, breasts, thighs, calves. His taste is a drug sending sparks dancing along every limb. I've craved it for months, needing it even as my heart hurt.

"Taylor. *My Starshine*," he pulls back, breathing heavily. "Are you sure?"

"I've wanted this since you stepped onto the ship four days ago." I'm breathless. Our chests are crushed together, nothing but the towel and his briefs between us.

"Me too, believe me." His forehead presses to mine and he whispers, voice uncertain, "But you've barely touched me until now."

"I needed to feel certain you weren't going to leave me behind again. And—"

"Never."

Our mouths meet and I bite his lip so hard he grunts, sealing his promise between us. The ice around my heart shatters.

My hands link behind his neck and I stare into his wide brown eyes. "And if I touched you — and I almost let myself, that morning — I wasn't sure I'd wait for that certainty, to know in my heart and my head that we're a team. Because I've missed this. You. Us."

He groans and his fingers dig into my skin. "I missed you too. So much."

"Show me."

His lips return to mine before I've finished speaking and he kisses me desperately. He turns, strides to the bed and sits on the edge, kissing me the entire time. I tug on my towel and it falls to the floor, then I crush our bodies together, feeling *right* as we press skin to skin. Like I'm home.

Still kissing, his palms glide up my back. My nipples rub over the coarse hair on his chest and I moan. I feel his hardness twitch and grind down against it, his briefs doing nothing to hide the heat of him. But I need them—

"Off." I say, sliding from his lap to tug them off.

He leans back on his hands and I stare at him, gulping air.

His arms and thighs are tense, muscles straining. His erection is thick and long. I bite my lip, my inner muscles clenching.

His own gaze glides over my body like it had that first day on the ship, the only difference now is the heat in his eyes, turning his gaze into a physical sensation moving over my face, neck, heavy breasts and hard nipples. The curve of my waist. The apex of my legs.

He grabs the back of my thighs and pulls me between his legs, his mouth latching onto a breast and sucking. I moan, tipping my head back, gripping his shoulders and swaying into him. He flicks his tongue over the hard nipple, cups the other breast in his hand and kneads.

"Riley," I gasp.

"I know. I know," he murmurs against my skin, kissing his way to the other breast, flicking his tongue over the bud, over and over until my nails dig into his shoulders.

"Move up." I push his chest and he goes willingly, dragging himself up the bed while I follow until I'm straddling him, braced over him on my elbows, kissing him again even as I speak. "I want you inside me."

"Later." An arm wraps around my torso and he spins us so I'm below him. His teeth graze the shell of my ear. "This first."

Then he kisses his way down my torso, fast, until he's between my thighs. His gaze goes hungry as he lifts my legs over his shoulders.

"I dreamed of tasting you every damn night we were apart," he growls, pressing kisses to my upper thighs.

He's not lying. He'd written about it in the letters I'd finally read last night.

He drops his head and we groan in tandem as he licks through my slick folds, straight up and over my swollen clit.

"I would've had you right there in the cargo bay that first day, if I thought you'd let me."

The shudder rips through my entire body. "I'm letting you now."

My hands curl and uncurl as he works his tongue over my clit, little flicks back and forth. It's not gentle. Every now and then, there's a hint of teeth. It rides the line between pleasure and pain but his warm hand travels over my thigh as a counterpoint and all too soon I'm at the edge of pleasure.

"Riley. *Oh gods.* I'm close. Can you—"

He hums against me and I whimper as he slides two fingers through my wetness, circling them at my entrance. He sucks hard on my clit and I'm gone, back bowing off the bed as I gasp, trembling as he keeps sucking until the pleasure-pain slides too far and I push his face away.

He grins at me, lips shiny and expression satisfied. I yank him on top of me with unsteady arms and kiss him.

"*Now* will you get inside me?"

He doesn't waste time with words, settling himself at my entrance and gliding in slow, giving me time to adjust, but I dig my heels into his lower back and push. I've waited months for my belief in us to be repaired. I'm not waiting another *second* now it has.

"Slow later," I tell him. "Fast now."

His eyes darken. "With pleasure."

He pulls almost all the way out then drives into me in one hard thrust. He curses. I gasp. Then he does it again. Again. Again. *Again.* Sliding against that part of me that makes my toes curl. We move together, bodies remembering each other as if no time has passed.

"Starshine." His eyes lock on mine. "I'm never leaving you behind again."

I whimper, my fingers digging into the muscles on his shoulder.

"Never." He kisses my neck. "Never." My collarbones. "*Never again.*" The slope of my breast.

Sweat builds on our skin, making the room smell of sex and vanilla and spice. I can't touch him enough. His sweat-slick back, the hard swells of his biceps, his neck, chest, ass. Our kisses are messy and my left foot slips off his back twice before he loops an arm around my leg and holds it against my chest. The angle drives him in deeper and a groan rips from me.

"You feel incredible." He shivers, head dropping to my neck. "I'm getting close."

"Me too. Together?"

"*Yes.* Touch yourself."

I cup his cheek and drop my hand to my clit, working myself as we stare, time stretching, becoming meaningless. It doesn't take long for my circling fingers to fling me skyward. He reads it on my face and in my body and shoves my leg wider, driving himself deeper inside me. Then he says my name and I break, free-falling through layers of pleasure, trembling as he follows me down, coming inside me, feeling each other's release like a feedback loop that intensifies until we're sharing the same pleasure, magnifying it.

He kisses me tenderly while we drift like feathers to the ground. My body is weightless but I feel grounded with Riley above me, whole and alive and mine.

He pulls out but doesn't go far. We lie facing each other on our sides, his hand on my hip, mine pressed to his chest over his heart.

"I'm sorry for leaving," he tells me again.

"I know. I forgive you."

We kiss lazily, letting heat build slowly until I feel him pressing against my hip and drift my hand down to circle him.

"The spacewalk?" he asks.

"It'll keep."

5
ALIEN MINE
DK HARRIS

ONE

Carrie glanced at the small group of soldiers as they walked up the wide hallway of the privately owned military compound outside the city of Insomnia. The planet was a bustling trade super-metropolis, the city itself spanning almost a quarter of the surface.

Humans had been granted entrance into the United Worlds Alliance decades earlier and she'd recently transferred from the earth-based university job she'd held for twelve years, to experience an alien culture firsthand.

Luckily, xenolinguists were in short supply and she'd been snaffled up as soon as her application went in. She'd been here only two weeks.

Assigned by the Earth Embassy to liaise with the owner of the compound to feel out the possibility of a soldier exchange in their elite training program, she'd found the handsome lekathian was married to a human, the first she'd come across outside the embassy.

The young human woman, Emma, linked her arm through Carrie's as they continued down the hall and chatted a mile a minute, her delight at seeing another human face obvious.

"I *have* to show you the VR training modules. They're incredible. You're actually *in* the program. The Earth Embassy is going to trip out completely when they see them." Emma dragged her toward an intersection of hallways, fast.

Carrie laughed and jogged to keep up. They hurtled around the corner.

"*Oomph!*" Carrie slammed face-first into a solid wall of muscle.

She stumbled and grabbed at the fabric covering that hard body so as not to fall flat on her ass.

"Watch it! Slow the fuck down. This isn't a fucking training track."

A rich, deep voice growled the words from above in Galactic Common, the main language of the UWA. Gentle but strong hands held her upright, regardless of the harshly spoken words.

"Don't be so antagonistic, cousin. Terran, are you okay?" a different, gentler voice asked from her right.

Carrie murmured a *yes*, regained her equilibrium and looked up.

And up.

Holy crap. This guy is huge!

He blocked out her vision. He had to be at least six foot seven, maybe taller, and broad across the shoulder. Muscles rippled on one bare arm. The other, up to and including his shoulder, was cybernetic, softly glowing amber lines tracing the joints. There didn't appear to be one ounce of wasted *anything* on his body.

Wow.

Longish black hair, shaved high on both sides of his head, with tiny braids on the sides that started at his temples and wound toward his crown, held it back from his face. A jagged scar ran across the back of one side of his head and down his neck to his cybernetic shoulder. Pale grey-blue skin. Bright aqua eyes glowed as they took her in as boldly as she herself was doing to him. He was built like a fucking Viking.

Highly pointed ears swept up, with two rings at the top on one side. A wide mouth with full, kissable lips sat below a straight nose. Lips that opened slightly, showing the sharp, longer points of his canines.

A shiver rippled down her spine. The sexy bastard had *fangs*.

Large hands ended in short, sharp, wicked-looking black claws. The cybernetic ones gleamed like obsidian. Combat pants, boots, and a vest covered his body.

"Sorry," she managed as she sucked in deep breath.

Sorry... not sorry?

The guy was edible. Totally and utterly delicious; with a side of violent, barely controlled malevolence that seemed to seep from his pores and surround him like a cloud.

Those impossibly beautiful eyes widened and he breathed in, going perfectly still.

"Who are you?" he rasped.

She hadn't taken her hands from his abdomen, couldn't seem to make them lift off his body.

"Carrie," she whispered.

A rumbling sigh left his lips, as if it was the answer to a long-held question.

Carrie squeaked as he lifted her, forcing her legs around his waist as he leaned into her neck and breathed deeply. She grabbed his shoulders to keep her balance. His chest expanded in a deep breath, and he rumbled louder.

What in hell was he doing?

"Why the fuck do you smell so damned good?"

The rough words peppered goosebumps down her spine and across every bit of skin on her body.

Dear God, the guy had the sexiest voice she'd ever heard. She tried to move slightly to ease the sudden throbbing ache between her thighs.

"Um... Can you put me down?"

He'd lifted her like she'd weighed nothing at all, and she wasn't petite. While short, she was curvy. She'd have fit into one of Rubens' paintings perfectly. Just with bigger boobs.

"*Hmm*," he murmured. "No."

He just stood there, his face buried in the crook of her neck. Carrie glanced down at Emma who stared at them, shock lacing her face.

Should she try to force him to put her down? She wasn't sure what species he was, and if resisting would trigger him.

The male brushed his lips up the side of her neck. She gasped. His lips skimmed her skin, his fangs scraping slightly, turning the goosebumps into full-on shivers. Without thinking she turned her head, as if to let him do whatever he wanted.

What the hell?

Why was she reacting like this? Why couldn't she think straight?

He breathed in again and a soft moan reached her ears. He slid his hands to her ass and gripped tight, squeezing her ass cheeks and pulling her snug against his pelvis. She clenched her hands around his neck as a shudder went clear down her spine at the hardness she felt between them.

"So fucking delicious," he growled.

Carrie dug her fingers into his shoulders at the unexpected sensation flooding her body. She wouldn't be surprised if her knickers were drenched from her unexpected arousal.

The guy was turning her on something fierce and all he'd done was *sniff* her.

"Nyx? Carrie is here on official business from the human embassy. Would you please put her down now?"

Emma's nervous voice made it to Carrie's ears.

"Nyx?" Carrie asked and slid her hand from his shoulder to cup his jaw. A nice name, that.

If Emma was anxious around him, the barely leashed hostility she'd felt surrounding him must be normal. She'd treat him carefully until she knew exactly what the hell was going on. He shuddered and lifted his head, his glazed eyes meeting hers. His slightly elongated fangs showed clearly in his parted mouth.

They looked so damned sexy. She wanted to kiss him — *hard*. The need was almost overwhelming.

"Say my name again," he demanded.

"Nyx," she whispered.

His vertical pupils widened, a dazed expression encompassing his face.

Why are you so damned gorgeous?

A huge grin widened his lush mouth.

Shit. Did I say that out loud?

He breathed in as if to speak, then his face changed, becoming almost feral in its intensity. He shoved her against the wall. Carrie squeaked in surprise.

One hand gripped her jaw, claws lightly pricking her skin. "I can smell your arousal for me, terran."

Caught between mortification as his words sank in, and shooting, extreme pleasure as his lips hit hers, Carrie slid her hands up the back of his neck and into his hair, unable to help herself.

His tongue plunged into her mouth and she gasped as he held her in place, devouring her. All thought dissipated. There was only him and his exquisite taste. Tiny pricks of his fangs teased her lips and she shuddered. She'd come just from his kiss if he kept it up much longer.

She'd never been kissed like this. Never been completely *owned* and destroyed by someone's mouth.

She gave it back as hard as he dished it out. He ground his hips into her, his incredibly hard, thick length pressed between her thighs, rubbing right where she wanted it. She pushed into the pressure, *needing* it.

"*Mine*." The guttural growl that sounded from him erupted goosebumps all over her.

"Nyx!" a male voice yelled.

He pulled sharply back, his head whipping to the side. Carrie stared at Nyx, wide-eyed, still dazed. She couldn't take her eyes from the alien who had just kissed her senseless.

"Put the terran down so she can breathe. You're about to swallow her whole."

CREW

Nyx's snarl at his cousin Volk's interruption had his lips curl back over his extended fangs. His gaze flicked off to his left to where he stood. His friends and fellow combat unit members all watched him warily, as if ready to jump in at a second's notice. He still gripped the terran's ass, holding her tight to his hips, his erection straining and actually painful, something he'd never experienced before.

He breathed deeply and fought the scent that swirled down deep into his blood.

Focus, dammit!

How could he think with that sweet, delicious scent teasing him, *begging* him?

It demanded he follow through and take the willing female in his arms, drown her in pleasure so intense that it might just kill them.

It demanded he claim her.

His eyes widened and he swore his heart clunked.

Claim? Where the fuck did that come from?

What the hell was he *doing*?

He looked back at the tiny terran in his arms.

Carrie.

Her name infused his blood, called to him on the basest level of his existence.

Carrie.

She looked at him with that same bewildered look he knew was on his own face. His gaze dropped to her full mouth, her swollen lips having that sensual, well-kissed appearance that twisted his gut in a tight knot.

He licked his bottom lip and shuddered at her lingering taste, then looked down to where his hands gripped her ass tightly.

"Shit. I'm sorry," he ground out.

He set her down carefully. Everything within him screamed not to let her go, instinct and desire vying for control with common sense.

Well, that's long-fucking gone, isn't it?

Common sense had nothing to do with what he'd just done, what he'd subjected her to. Someone he'd barely gotten the name of before he'd tried to rut her in the hallway like some freaking animal.

He held her waist until it looked like she could stand by herself and forced himself to step away from temptation, because she tempted the hell out of him even now. He knew all it would take would be one look from her to be right back where they'd been moments ago, and he wouldn't give a damn who was watching as he took her against the wall.

No. He couldn't submit to that. That was... *wrong*.

What the hell had come over him?

He dared risk a glance at her again. "I'm sorry. I don't... I don't know what happened."

Liar.

He knew his head injury had knocked some screws loose, but surely he wasn't that far gone he'd force a female?

She doesn't look too forced to me.

Shut the fuck up!

He shook his head at his internal argument and retreated another step. Carrie leaned against the wall, extreme embarrassment replacing the confusion on her face. She couldn't hold his gaze. She looked at the floor and shrugged.

"It's fine. I, uh... It's fine," she repeated.

Her delicious, soft voice sent goosebumps skittering over his entire form.

It wasn't fine, not at all. He was better than this.

He placed a shaking hand over his heart and lowered his gaze to the floor. A gesture of supplication to Carrie, a remnant from his past, one he'd never willingly made.

He turned and stalked off down the opposite hall, needing to get away from what he'd done, and the life-changing realization that had hit him, causing him to act so out of character. The pressure of the assessing eyes on his back watching his retreat made his skin crawl.

He knew exactly what had happened, and it scared the living shit out of him.

TWO

"Why did Nyx react like that? Why did he *sniff* me? Why did he say *mine*?"

Carrie turned at her open front door and touched Volk's muscled forearm, desperate for an answer. He'd driven her home in a military hovercar.

Why did I react the way I did?

Volk stiffened and bit his lip, frowning. He looked concerned, but strangely, also hopeful. He was a gentle male, softly spoken and kind.

"Nyx... is my cousin. He's often intense, but not usually savage." He scrubbed his jaw. "You've heard of lifemates amongst the alien species in this galaxy?" He waited until she nodded. "It's incredibly rare. Most of us are resigned to the fact that we'll never know that kind of connection, that love. It's detectable by scent and this deep-seated *knowing*. Knowing that one person is *yours* and you are theirs. It's biology at the deepest level.

"Nyx keeps himself apart from almost everyone. The only ones he lets remotely close are our unit." Volk looked at her, shock and awe vying for supremacy on his face. "Today, with you? That was..." He sucked in a deep breath. "I have no doubt what I witnessed today was the recognition of that bond between you both. Orin sent him out on an errand to give him something to focus on while he processes what's happened."

Carrie pressed a shaking hand to her chest and blew out a breath, shock flooding her blood.

A lifemate bond. With an alien.

She shook her head. How could that be? She'd completely lost all sense of self when Nyx had looked at her, when he'd kissed her. All she'd wanted was him. It had consumed her.

She'd heard of lifemates. It was spoken about in hushed tones between the alien races, a thing so sacrosanct that it had been referenced and studied even on Earth.

To be honest, she hadn't really believed the stories.

It had seemed too fanciful, too contrived. Too perfect.

"But I'm human. How is that possible?"

Volk held up his hands and shook his head. Did she even want something like that? She'd divorced over a decade ago, focusing on her career. She'd had no plans to date, let alone what *lifemates* implied.

"Is it inevitable?"

"Yes and no. The bond can be ignored or refused. But deep down it's always inside you, aching for that other half of your soul, begging fulfilment. It never truly goes away if you've met them and refuse it." Volk smiled sadly and looked truly apologetic. "I know it's unexpected, and probably scary as hell, but... maybe just give him a chance?"

He smiled awkwardly, stepped back into the hallway, and pulled the door shut behind him.

CBED

Carrie scrubbed her short hair with a towel and walked into her living room, her shower-dampened body wrapped in another.

She touched her bottom lip and a shiver coursed over her.

Nyx had tasted *so good.*

She hadn't seen him the rest of her visit to the compound. She wasn't sure if she was relieved, or really annoyed that Orin had sent him away. She perched on the rolled arm of her sofa and rubbed the lingering moisture from her hair.

Lightning flashed outside her huge living room window. The close-following thunder made her jump. It had been raining for hours now. The wet season had well and truly hit. Insomnia had two seasons — cold and wet, or hot and dry.

A sharp rap of knuckles against her apartment door startled her. Carrie glanced at the clock. Eleven o'clock.

Who would be visiting at such an hour? Security in her building was tight. Emma was the only person she'd given her access and floor code to, in case she wanted to visit with another human in the alien city.

She opened the door and her heart stuttered as a bedraggled and dripping-wet Nyx filled her doorway. His hands dug deep in his back pockets and he bit his bottom lip, sucking it into his mouth. It was such a human pose that she almost laughed.

"Can I..." He scraped a clawed hand through his hair and looked as if he was about to puke from nervousness. "Would I be able to come in?"

His rich voice sent goosebumps all over her. Carrie blinked and stepped back.

"Of course. You're drenched, I'll get you a towel."

He stepped through the doorway and scanned the room as she handed him the towel she'd used on her hair. He wiped his wet face, then swore under his breath, his eyes closing as he breathed deep into the fabric.

Dammit. She hadn't thought of the scent thing.

"I'll get you a clean one." She turned to hurry to the bathroom.

"No. This one is perfect."

She faced him and saw the instant he realized she wore only a towel. Carrie stood straighter. She refused to feel self-conscious. He'd come to her home late at night; he'd have to deal with it.

That same rumbling growl that had gotten her so aroused earlier washed over her.

How was she going to resist him? Did she even want to?

He removed his wet boots without taking his gaze from her. She knew he couldn't see anything, that the towel covered her from chest to knee, but it didn't stop her feeling like he'd stripped her bare and was devouring her visually.

He straightened as more thunder ripped the sky. Carrie jumped again, so focused on him that she'd forgotten the wild storm outside.

"Is my ma..." Nyx cut off his words, frowned, and started again. "Are *you* scared of storms?"

She shook her head. He'd been going to say *mate.*

"Not usually. They're just a bit noisier here than on Earth."

He moved toward her carefully, slowly, as if she were a skittish animal in the sights of a predator.

She almost laughed at that. He was an apex predator, and she hoped he'd catch *her.*

"I realize it's late, but I wanted to apologize properly for my behaviour this morning. It was inexcusable. I treated you like a, a *thing,* and it's been chewing at me all afternoon."

Carrie gestured to the sofa and sat at the far end. "It really is okay. Volk explained. So, I get it, even though it's rather confronting."

Nyx sat carefully, slowly easing himself into the seat.

He dominated the room. His sheer size overpowered the three-seater sofa.

"I would like to introduce myself and, if you're willing, get to know you. This is all a bit..." He scraped those claws through his hair again and shook his head. "Fuck. It's crazy is what it is."

He looked at her and sucked in a ragged breath. The intensity in his gorgeous aqua eyes sent shivers skittering over her spine.

"I look at you and all I can think of is how can I get you out of that towel and under me. It's consuming me."

Her gut tumbled at his honesty. Carrie bit her lip, suddenly nervous at her circling thoughts, at the thought that she really wouldn't mind that at all. "Would it help to do something about it? Would that relieve anything?"

His piercing gaze narrowed in on her. She felt as if nothing else existed in the universe in that moment, other than them.

She tried to smile at him. It came out wonky and lopsided. "I mean, I'm sure it's no secret that I find you incredibly attractive. You make me want..." She shrugged a shoulder. "Well, let's just say things I haven't wanted in a long time."

"You want...?" He motioned between them.

She nodded. Her heart wanted to explode at the hopeful yet panicked expression on his face.

"But I'm too big for a terran. For you. How would that even work? I would damage you."

"You'd be surprised how flexible and accommodating the human body is. Orin is almost your size and Emma's only a few inches taller than me. They haven't had any problems in that area."

Or, so Emma had promised.

He released a sharp growl and pounced. She fell back into the soft cushioning as his mouth hit hers. His taste hit her, flooded her in need. She grabbed him and opened her mouth. He cupped her head. Strangely, his cybernetic hand was as warm as his real one. Carrie shifted beneath him and ran her leg up his thigh, trying to get him to a more comfortable position.

Who was she kidding? She wanted him on top of her.

Nyx groaned into her mouth. "It would destroy me if I hurt you."

He touched, stroked, and slid his hands over the outside of the towel, obvious need overruling his words.

She wiggled and the towel tugged open. She grabbed his hand and placed it on her breast, her other one buried deep in his hair. "You won't. I know you won't."

He kissed and licked down her neck, then across to her breast, sucking her nipple into his mouth. His fangs rasped over the hard nub. Her gasp was loud enough to overcome his growl.

He dragged his mouth from her breast. Lust-glazed aqua eyes stared into her own.

So damned pretty.

"I didn't come here expecting anything other than to meet you properly. You don't have to do this."

"I want you, Nyx. We can work the rest out later."

He cupped her head in a large hand, barely leashed malevolence swirling in his eyes. "That's just it — if we do this, it's an acceptance of the bond. Our bodies won't know the difference, even if our minds aren't there yet. You'll be bound to me. I won't do that to you unless you're certain. No matter how much it kills me not being inside you right now." He closed those beautiful eyes and rested his forehead against hers. "I can't ask that of you, not when we barely know each other."

Butterflies flocked her stomach. Acceptance spread like fire through her blood, saturating every nerve and cell. "I *want* you. Apparently now we've met I'm going to want you for eternity." She licked the top of his ear. He gasped and bucked against her.

"Take me to bed. Now."

He shuddered, grabbed her, and stumbled to her bedroom. He laid her down and ripped his clothes from his body, then kneeled over her. His right leg and hip were the same as his left arm — high-tech cybernetics.

Her mate was a cyborg. Part machine, part organic.

Carrie devoured him with her eyes and hands. She couldn't stop touching him. Each touch elicited a moan, a gasp. Both his nipples were pierced with thick rings. She looked lower.

Long and heavy, his cock strained erect and thick. A chunky bar-piercing speared him just beneath the crown. Small nodules ran the length of him, top and bottom.

Oh, boy.

She swallowed. She was actually salivating at the sight of him naked.

"Like what you see?" he rasped.

Carrie nodded, not trusting her voice to work.

"I want to take my time, to make you scream with pleasure, but I, I don't know how long I can last. I *need* you."

Carrie grabbed his hand and pushed his fingers between her legs, desperate to feel any part of him there. She bit her lip to contain her moan as Nyx stroked her. He pulled his fingers from her and licked them, groaning.

Carrie wrapped her hand around as much of his base she could and squeezed through the stroke.

He bucked against her hand and swore, breathing heavily, visibly trying to hold it together. His organic arm trembled, his face tight with determination and need.

"Are you sure?" he whispered. Intense aqua eyes stared into her own. Her heart wanted to burst that he would give her an out, even now.

"Yes."

She lifted her hips so that he touched her. He took the hint and pushed forward. Neither of them breathed as his broad tip pierced her. He flexed his hips. Her eyes closed and she gasped as he stopped just inside her; so thick, so filling.

"Look at me."

Her eyes fluttered open. He held himself still, body strung tight with the control it took not to move while she got used to his size. He rocked, pushing a little deeper. He swore, his face contorted with concentration, and rocked some more.

"*Carrie...*"

Hearing her name on his lips broke something inside her. She grabbed his hips and pulled hard.

Nyx moaned and thrust, seemingly unable to help himself, filling her completely. Carrie cried out and grabbed his shoulders as he pumped into her. The burn of him stretching her lasted but a moment, exquisite pleasure flooding her with his heat as he moved.

She sucked his nipple ring into her mouth and tugged. Nyx gasped and bucked. Muscles, hard and sweat-sheened, bunched and contracted around her. She scraped her nails down his sides and wrapped her legs around his hips.

He was perfection.

Scars, small and large, peppered the skin beneath her hands and mouth, not detracting from his appeal. If anything, it made her hotter for him.

He slid a hand between them and stroked that sensitive nub of nerves. Carrie cried out and jerked against him.

Oh *yes*.

"*There*," she gasped.

He did it again. She dug her nails into his skin. Nyx growled and shoved himself backward onto his knees. His large, strong hands lifted her hips as he widened his legs, keeping his length firmly inside her. He cupped her ass in his hands and started to pump hard.

Carrie whimpered, the pleasure too much. Each stroke, each thrust, the mixture of his size, his feel, clashed and swirled into a typhoon of ecstasy.

"Nyx!" she gasped, gripping the sheets, twisting them tight in her fists as she was splayed out before him, her thighs wide over his.

He bucked and jerked in his steady rhythm. One hand left her ass, and his fingers found her clit, circling, sliding; the other holding her tight on him, claws pricking her skin.

Carrie fell apart.

She screamed as he worked her, his fingers and cock driving her ever higher, forcing her to feel *more* as wave after wave of bliss flooded her, owned her. She clamped tight on him and he stiffened. His back arched as he roared, his fangs elongated and bared as he came hard, spilling inside her. He ground against her, his breaths ragged, gasping.

Carrie's eyes flew open at sudden, sharp pain at the juncture of her neck and shoulder. Nyx curved over her, one arm braced by her head, his fangs buried deep.

She fisted his hair tight, unsure whether to pull him away or hold him there. Her core suddenly clenched around him as liquid fire flooded her veins. Utter bliss washed through her blood, sinuous and alive.

Orgasm hit again in a sudden wave. Harder. So intense she couldn't breathe. Carrie cried out into his neck, her voice hoarse. She gasped against his skin, desperate for air.

Wave after wave of torturous pleasure swamped her, almost too much to bear. Her hands and legs fell limp to the bed. She couldn't move. Didn't think she ever would again.

Nyx lifted his head and licked at her shoulder, causing slight shudders to shimmer over her skin emanating from that point. He trembled above her, then rolled onto his back, carrying her with him, his cock still buried deep.

Shaking hands stroked her fevered flesh.

"Carrie? *Ayvara*?"

His croaky voice pierced her pleasure-saturated brain. She slid her hand up his chest to rest near her face. She sprawled boneless on top of him.

"Hmm?"

A soft chuckle reached her ears. He slid his hands over her ass and squeezed, moaning softly to himself.

"You are everything I never let myself wish for," Nyx whispered.

Carrie breathed deep to control the sudden emotion suffusing her. She lifted her head and he smiled gently and stroked her ass again. "You are so soft, yet so strong. I don't know how it's possible, but we fit so perfectly."

He cupped her jaw. The reverence in his gaze was almost too much. Carrie bit her lip.

"It was pretty intense. Transcendent."

He pushed her short hair from her forehead then touched the spot where he'd bitten her. "I'm sorry I didn't think to warn you of this. My fangs have never descended before. It wasn't a conscious thought."

Carrie propped her chin on the back of her hand. "I won't lie, it hurt; but whatever you have running in those fangs packs one hell of an orgasmic punch. I'm pretty sure I could forgive you anything to feel that."

Relief and more than a little smug pride laced his grin. His fangs had receded, although not back to the position they'd been in when she'd first met him that morning. He touched his tongue to one. Pleasure momentarily brightened his eyes and his cock twitched inside her.

"I licked the holes to close them. It should heal fully overnight. It's called venom, even though it's not poisonous. It's a biological gift for your lifemate."

And what a gift it was.

Carrie reached up to touch a long, jagged scar across the back of his head that led down his neck and reached to his shoulder. Nyx's eyes darkened at her silent question.

"Volk and I were in an elite tactical unit for the Vorallian Consect. He tells me we were counterintelligence. I was injured in a drop we did about three years ago. We went in to retrieve an important asset who'd been kidnapped. It was a set up — leaked info to dispose of our unit. I should've died. It's how I ended up with these." He tapped a cybernetic prosthesis. "I have plates in my head, as well. I lost a good whack of my memory. Bits and pieces sometimes bleed through. Orin was a close friend of mine from the academy. When he heard about what happened, he offered both Volk and I a position here, with his unit."

He ran a claw down her cheek, seemingly unable to stop touching her. "That unit is my life. I have no immediate family, Volk and his are it. Most of the memories that remain include him. What you see is what you get." He dropped his gaze, but not before she saw shame flicker in his eyes. "I don't have much to offer. I'm sorry your lifemate is such a mess."

Carrie pushed up on her arms and looked at him. "There's nothing to be sorry *for*. I see a male who lost almost everything — including his life — in service to his government. I'd say that's pretty exceptional, wouldn't you?"

She rubbed her thumb over his bottom lip, lips that parted at the sensation.

"Take me out tomorrow night, because I think I'd like to date you."

Nyx laughed and rolled her over, settling between her thighs, that lingering shame disappearing from his eyes. "I'd like that." He nuzzled her neck and moaned. "Anything to make you happy, *ayvara*. Anything."

Carrie grinned and tilted her head to give him better access. "What does that word mean?"

He licked up to her ear. "It means *my life*."

Carrie stroked his hair. It looked like *her* life had just got a hell of a lot more interesting.

6

MACHINE MAN

KRISTIN SILK

Sess-sha

Sweet Maya.

The beast is as big as a bancha. But deadlier. It rumbles, roars and shakes the earth, leaving a trail of destruction in its wake. Sunlight glints off its silvery hide as if it were a precious jewel rather than the destroyer of my home and the killer of my people.

Vibrations echo through my bare feet as I cling to my branch, high in a tree at the edge of the forest. The beast heaves with a screeching groan, sinking its teeth into the earth, tearing out huge chunks. It twists, dumping the contents in a growing pile.

The surrounding earth is flattened. Trees ripped out by the roots, tossed aside as if by a vicious wind. Mounds of dirt replace lush green plants and the animals who lived here. Smaller metallic creatures roll around beside the beast, as if they are doing its bidding.

My chest aches. Why do they come and kill and lay our lands to waste?

I know what they are, even if I've never seen one.

Shining devils. Destroyers.

Intermittently, the smaller beasts pause, releasing shiny figures from their bellies. My eyes widen. They carry their young inside? So destructive and yet maternal? A strange contradiction.

The largest beast screeches again. I shiver and melt back into the trees.

∞

Sess-sha

At the far side of the forest, a flash of light blinds me.

Blinking rapidly, I reach for my bow.

One of the smaller creatures lies on its side, sunlight dancing off its silver body. Its circular feet lie still. It's a long way from the others, who stay close to the starships that brought them to our lands.

I scan in all directions, listening intently. Sniff the air. Safe. For now.

But the creature itself is a threat I can't leave unchecked. I pick my way towards it.

It doesn't move or make a sound as I approach.

Warily, I tap the plated armour. Cold. Deathly cold.

I crawl up the side. A hard silver spur sticks out of the beast's armour plate. I tug. It twists down and the whole section peels open with a strange whirring sound, exposing the cavity of the destroyer's belly. I freeze but the creature doesn't respond.

The interior is the same silver as the outside, with rows of buttons and square panels. But it's what lies at the bottom of the beast's belly that snags my attention.

Offspring.

Is it alive? Encased in shiny skin? I can't tell.

I prop the armour plate open and climb inside, keeping a wary distance from the beast's young.

Unlike the squat, indistinct mass of the adults, the juvenile destroyer has arms, legs and a head.

Pulling my hunting knife from my belt, I poke its leg.

It cries out, smooth head turning in my direction.

I leap back with a hiss, knife braced, ready.

We stare at each other for long moments. My pulse thunders in my ears.

Then it speaks, in the common tongue. "Don't kill me."

Shining devils can talk? "Don't give me reason to."

"I won't hurt you."

We stare at each other some more.

"Help me?" The offspring tugs at its head. Is it injured? Grieving the loss of its parent, which I'm now sure is deceased? "Please."

It wants to dismember itself? Perhaps distress has bypassed all reason.

"You want to tear off your head?"

"Not head. Helmet," comes the muffled reply. "Hard to breathe."

Sheathing my knife, I move closer, poking the dazzlingly bright skin. Cold and hard like its dead parent.

Despite my misgivings, I assist. The creature's head slides up, then comes right off.

I gasp. There's a face underneath, with deep brown skin, high cheek bones and full lips.

"Thank you." The offspring's rich, deep voice resonates low in my belly.

Dark eyes framed with thick lashes stare up at me. A strange sensation pulses in my chest, as if something inside me has clicked into place and locked there. My gaze falls to the creature's lips. An unsettling prickle of awareness sweeps through me.

Those sensuous lips curve up. "Hello."

It looks like Moragai, apart from its silver body. I stroke a tentative finger over the beads of sweat on its forehead. It feels like skin. Like me. My body hums and tingles at the contact. I pull my hand away.

"I'm sorry for the loss of your parent." Even if one less shining devil is a good thing for my planet.

"What?"

I gesture around me. "Your parent did not survive."

A pause. "Not my parent. It's a vehicle, a means of travelling from one place to another. A machine."

"Machine." I frown. "If you are not the shining devil's offspring, then what are you?"

The creature presses a palm to its chest. "Human. Man."

"Hoomanman?"

"Species: Human. Gender: Male. Name: Malachai."

"Malachai." My tongue stumbles over the delicious tumble of syllables.

"And you are?"

"Species: Moragai. Gender: Female. Name: Sess-sha."

"Sess-sha." The way he says it, drawing out the s's makes my belly tingle. "Pleased to meet you." His smile makes my blood pump faster. I don't like the sensation but return his smile before my brain catches up.

"Could you help me get this off? It's uncomfortable." He gestures to the rest of his shiny skin.

"What is it?"

"Armour, for protection."

Protection? Why would he need that? Nothing can stand against the destroyers.

I pull at the shining metal plate that covers his torso. It comes loose, revealing a grey top, soaked with sweat, stretched over a broad muscled chest. Oh. My mouth goes dry.

His lips turn up in a knowing smile at my reaction.

My cheeks heat. I refocus on my task, pulling the hard silver coating off, revealing clothing and warm skin underneath.

When I get to his right leg, he hisses. I ease the armour off as gently as I can. The gash on his thigh is deep. Blood pools beneath it.

I wince. He's too big to carry, too injured to travel quickly. Others will come soon, and darkness is approaching.

Standing, I peer out the propped open space. In the distance a bancha howls. My skin prickles. I can't linger.

I climb part way out and sniff the air. Bancha's not close enough to smell, but still, too close. They will smell blood soon enough and the machine man will be bancha food. So will I, if I stay here.

You owe him nothing. Leave him.

Mancha duria. The thought intrudes. But surely it doesn't apply to my enemy?

He watches me, eyes pinched with pain, expression resigned, as if he can read my thoughts.

He's weak. If banchas don't get him, scavengers will. He won't last the night.

The strange tug in my chest pulls tighter, as if I'm bound to him in some inexplicable way, as if he's mine now.

Mancha duria. If I turn away from his suffering, I'm no better than the shining devils who wreak such havoc on our peaceful planet.

I sigh, cursing my conscience. "Can you sit?"

The flash of hope in his eyes is a tiny, fragile thing.

He struggles up.

I ease him into a standing position, arm around his waist. He sways. "Just... give me a moment." He forces the words through a clenched jaw.

We don't have a moment. The bancha howls again, closer this time. "Come." My voice is urgent. "Come now."

છ૪ૐ

Malachai

A thousand white hot needles stab my leg. My head spins with every step. I'm grateful she didn't leave me, but... "I can't."

"Can," she counters. "Keep going."

I'm weak as a newborn kitten. Sweating and shaking. And the pain. *Fuck.* Tears wet my cheeks. I can't go on. But I won't take her down with me. "Leave me."

"No. Come on. *Move.*"

She's a drill sergeant, her stubborn determination a pain in the arse. She's also the only thing keeping me alive right now.

I struggle onward, focussing on her voice, on the strong grip of the slender arm around my waist. The forest is a green blur.

One foot forward. A harsh breath. *Another.*

"Keep going. Again. Again."

Just when I think I can't walk another step, we reach a huge tree. "Up." She points to steps carved into the massive trunk.

You've got to be fucking kidding me. I shake my head. My vision blurs.

She sighs, then pulls on a thick rope made of vines. A harness descends. She straps me in and disappears up the tree. Then I'm being hauled up, the ground disappearing below me. How is she lifting me? She's half my size and I'm a dead weight.

A pulley system made of... plants levers the swing up. A primitive machine. I hang on for dear life. Finally, she pulls me onto a platform and frees me from the harness.

I crawl the remaining distance into a treehouse.

Something howls in the forest. The hairs on the back of my neck rise. "What's that?"

"Bancha. Native carnivore." She grins, a flash of white teeth against her light brown skin. "Don't worry. Big, but can't climb."

She eases me onto a mattress. Her dark braids tickle my arms as she pulls the cover over me. She could be human except for the pointed ears and the golden glow of her eyes. *Beautiful.*

My pulse stutters as I meet her gaze, transfixed. The strange feeling from before returns, like everything in me has rearranged and oriented towards her. It's powerful. I want to stare into her eyes forever.

Careful fingers stroke my forehead. "Rest now."

Her kindness and the pain conspire against me. Tears trickle down my cheeks.

She makes a soft, crooning noise, gently wiping my face. "Mancha duria. I will not leave you. Rest."

A strange sense of safety settles over me. My eyelids close as she continues to stroke my hair, her compassion wrapping me like a blanket.

ᘓᔓᔔᘔ

Sess-sha

Malachai is unconscious. He was too weak to reach my dwelling, so I brought him here, to one of the hunters' communal huts. His dark skin burns as he sweats and trembles with fever. I don't know how long he's been injured but I need to clean the wound.

As I cut off his bloody clothes with my knife, my eyes widen. His cock nestles in a nest of black curls, big, even in its resting state.

I swallow hard. *Focus.*

After washing his wound, I apply a healing balm and wrap it with mallow leaves. When he wakes, briefly, I feed him a tonic to kill the infection. His throat works in clumsy gulps as he swallows.

This intense connection demands I care for him as if he's my own and give him whatever he needs.

Madness. He's the enemy.

But my heart overrides my thoughts with a strange new beat. *Mine*, it pulses. *Mine.*

ය⋙

Malachai

A damp cloth slides over my face and neck, scented with something sweet and herby. There's a small slosh as the cloth is dipped back in water. Firm hands gently lift one of my arms. The cloth moves down to my fingers in rhythmic, circular motions. Am I dead? Is this an angel? Do they wash you in Heaven?

I surrender completely to the blissful touch. The angel strokes the damp cloth over my other arm, a sensual caress. My leg throbs with a dull ache but the burning fire is gone.

The cloth glides over my chest and stomach, followed by fingers lightly stroking. Oh, that feels good. So good.

Too good.

My eyes snap open. A woman with dark hair and golden eyes leans over me, smiling. "Welcome back."

What? Where am I? I stare up at branches and leaves.

Then, memory hits me. The malfunction of my metal pod. The crash. The woman who saved me. *Sess-sha.* "How long have I been asleep?"

"Three days."

Holy shit. How is that even possible?

She continues to slide the cloth over my stomach. "Infection has passed." My cock twitches to life and I stare down at myself. Naked with a semi. *Christ.*

Her gaze fixes on my cock, too, lips twitching. "Optimistic. You must be feeling better."

I bark out an embarrassed laugh.

"When you're well enough, I'll take you to the waterhole. But for now, this will have to do."

Sess-sha slides the cloth down my good leg. She carefully washes my sore leg, working her way upwards, parting my thighs so she can get better access. She washes between my legs with no hint of embarrassment. I suck in a shaky breath as she strokes the cloth over my now fully hard and aching cock and my balls. A strangled whimper escapes me.

She stills. "Is this alright? Sorry. I would have asked, but you were asleep." Uncertainty flashes in her eyes. "I thought you should be clean."

"It's more than okay." It's been so long since anyone touched me so gently and pleasurably. The hunger is overwhelming.

She had no reason to help me. She could have left me to die. Given the way we've treated her people and her planet, I wouldn't blame her. Yet she brought me to safety, cared for me. For *three days.* Lord knows washing me in my current state is not a task for the faint hearted.

My throat tightens at her kindness. "Thank you."

"Mancha duria." She returns her cloth to the water bowl and shuffles closer.

The pull towards her is intense, even in my weakened state. I reach for her hand.

Our fingers entwine and our gazes lock. Her other hand strokes my face, neck and torso, soothing and gentle. Her touch sets me on fire.

Energy pulses between us like a living thing. As she stares into my eyes, I have the strangest thoughts. *I found you. I'm home.*

I don't know what this is, but I don't want it to end. My skin tingles and I crave her touch. My cock throbs and aches.

"How is your leg?"

"Sore but not as bad."

Gentle fingers trace circles over my chest. "Is this alright?"

"Yes. It... feels good." My voice comes out deeper than usual. 'Good' is a fucking understatement.

"The pain will ease in a day or so."

"I'm guessing you don't have painkillers here?"

She frowns. "My medicines are doing their job."

Now I feel like an arsehole. "I appreciate you looking after me."

"But you are in pain?"

"A bit. But not like before."

She bites her lip, deep in thought. My gaze falls to her mouth. How is it possible that I get even harder? I want her more than I've ever wanted anyone.

"I could..." She shakes her head, lowering her eyes, cheeks darkening.

I squeeze her hand gently. "What? You can tell me."

"Pleasure might cancel out the pain."

My cock twitches hopefully. Surely that's not what she meant.

She stares at my chest, then meets my gaze. "I could... touch you, here, if you like. Give you something else to focus on?" She waves her hand above my cock. It jerks like she's stroking it.

A beautiful woman offering to touch my cock? I'm dead for sure. Maybe this is Heaven after all.

"Or... not?"

I stare at her, open mouthed, like a muppet. "Yeah. Sure. You can... touch me there. Yes. Please." *Christ. Really fucking cool, man.* My cheeks burn.

She presses her fingers to my lips. *Yeah. Good call.* Her eyes dance with amusement as she reaches for a bottle of fragrant oil and pours a slug into her hand. Worry flickers through me. It's been a while. What if I embarrass myself?

"No moving. Your leg needs rest."

I nod. She massages my stomach and along my inner thighs. When she grips my cock between slippery fingers, I suck in a sharp breath.

Then, she gently kneads my balls. *Oh god.*

She slowly strokes me from base to tip and I release a jagged breath. Pleasure ripples through me.

"You like this?"

"Yeah." The word comes out jerky as if it has more than one syllable.

Golden eyes lock on mine as she pumps me slowly. It's been so long since anyone touched me this way and it feels *sooo good.*

My breath is rough. I groan helplessly.

Energy sparks between us. Intense. I've never felt anything like it. Her gaze holds me prisoner. I surrender willingly.

"How's your leg?"

"What leg?"

Her reply is a low, sexy chuckle.

"Can I touch you, too?"

She nods, using one hand to stroke me while the thumb of her other hand traces my lips. I suck her thumb into my mouth. Her eyes widen.

I slide my hand up her thigh, then up over her breast, stroking her nipple through her top while I suck on her thumb. Her breath hitches but her massage doesn't falter.

Lightning builds at the base of my spine. The ache is urgent. When I try to thrust into her hand, she removes her thumb from my mouth, pressing my hips down. "No moving or I'll stop."

I whimper. Please don't ever stop. Fuck. *Oh my fucking god.* I tremble uncontrollably, the pleasure's so intense it's almost pain.

She pumps harder, faster. I stiffen, the need in me like a tightly coiled spring threatening to explode.

There's nothing but the sound of my gasping breaths, the rude wet noises as she pumps me, using both hands now.

"Relax, masai mendurak. Let the pleasure take you."

I give in, trusting her completely.

Then.

Ohmyfuckinggod. Fire explodes in my balls, shooting up into my cock. I let out a strangled cry as I jerk and come so hard I see stars, my release spurting over my stomach in hot bursts.

I lie gasping, staring at the leaf canopy in a daze, my body wracked with aftershocks of pleasure. Everything inside me has been rearranged, now focussed on her like a heat-seeking missile.

What the hell just happened?

Her soft smile causes a melting sensation in my chest. After gently wiping away my release, she leans forward to kiss my stomach.

We stare at each other. Time ceases as the moment stretches. Though I'm physically sated, a part of me still aches. For her.

"Can I give you pleasure too?"

With a nod, she removes her clothing, revealing acres of light brown skin. *Fuck, she's gorgeous.*

She straddles my stomach, carefully avoiding my leg. "Don't exert yourself too much. You're still healing."

When I stroke my hands over her soft skin, she sighs. I caress her stomach, gliding up to cup her breasts, capturing her brown nipples between my fingers and squeezing gently until she gasps.

My heart pounds at her responsiveness. "Kiss me?"

The press of her mouth against mine is not tentative or shy. It's a breath of fire, setting me alight. I kiss her back hungrily, wishing I was fully functional.

As she plunders my mouth, I stroke eager hands over her back, pulling her closer. The way her arse fits perfectly in my palms is a revelation, the soft skin of her thighs the answer to a prayer.

I slide my fingers down through the dark curls between her legs, into her slick folds.

When I circle her swollen bud, her breath hitches.

"More?"

"*Yes.*"

She moans, grinding her mound against my hand, seeking

friction. I press a finger inside her, then glide the slick arousal over her clit.

Her needy whimper spurs me on. Adding another finger, I pump into her slick, wet heat.

She bites my earlobe, her breath harsh in my ear.

I urge her higher so I can suck on her breasts, alternating each nipple while my fingers work inside her.

As she starts to tremble, a rush of satisfaction spears me. I want to see her come apart and to be the cause of it.

Her mouth is parted, her eyes closed. She's completely focussed on her pleasure and it's hot as hell. I speed up my movements. She makes the sexiest noises, little gasps and cries as she moves against my hand.

Then, her eyes snap open, staring into mine with breathtaking intensity. Like she owns me. Like she's claiming me with her eyes. Her thighs shake, then her whole body joins in. Her face twists in pleasure.

She breaks with a loud cry, muscles clenching around my fingers. I keep stroking until she gently stills my hand, sagging against me.

When she presses her face into my neck, I hold on tight. The weight of her is comforting as I stroke her back gently while she comes down.

Too soon, she eases off me and lies against my side. I wrap my arms around her and kiss her. Her smile is adorable, a little shy. She was so sexy and confident that the hint of vulnerability takes me by surprise. It only makes me want her more.

We caress each other's faces. "Rest now." Her voice is husky and sexy as hell.

The pain has almost completely gone. I drift off to sleep with a smile on my face.

෴

Malachai

These weeks with Sess-sha have been the best of my life. Every day she blows me away with her kindness and strength. We haven't been intimate since that first time, but we cuddle every night. I'm not sure what that means.

I wear the traditional dress of her people. A skirt the size of a handtowel that barely covers my junk. A little confronting at first, but the way her eyes fix on my bare chest has me flexing my arms and rolling back my shoulders like a peacock.

Aiming my bow towards the target, I shoot, and miss.

Sess-sha gives me a knowing smile. "You are strong, but you need to work on your aim."

I collect my arrow.

She aims, her lithe limbs in perfect symmetry. She wears a small skirt made of animal pelts and a top that criss-crosses over her breasts. They do little to hide her luscious brown skin. I want to trace every inch of that skin with my mouth. Ah, crap. *Down boy.*

She hits the target perfectly. Three times. Of course, she does. She's incredible.

Our connection is intense, the need for her a constant ache. I've fallen hard, and desperately want her to fall back.

But what am I to her? A one off means to scratch an itch? A wounded animal to be released back into the wild after recovery? More?

"Sess-sha?"

"Mmm?"

"What's mancha duria?"

She pauses, flicking her dark braid over one shoulder.

"It means 'I see the light in you'. To my people it means, when you see a soul in need, you don't look away from their suffering."

My stomach sinks. Is that all I am to her? "Like a burden? A responsibility?"

A wrinkle mars her forehead. "Responsibility, yes. Burden, no. It is an honour and a privilege to aid a soul in need."

When I lay bleeding out in my pod, the comms system tuned in to central control before it fritzed. I could hear them. They couldn't hear me.

"Control. Pod 51 is down."

A pause, then the reply. "Cut him loose."

In other words, leave me to die.

Sess-sha's golden eyes search mine. "Don't your people have such a thing?"

A humourless laugh escapes me. "No. They don't."

I was nothing but a cog in a machine powered by insatiable greed. They threw me away like a broken part once I failed to be useful. Sess-sha's beautiful homeland only had value to them if they destroyed it. And for what? So a few rich arseholes can keep getting richer? Well, fuck that.

Sess-sha

I brace my arms on the rock in front of me, acutely aware of Malachai at my back.

We stare at the starships. Machines, he calls them. Made of parts but not alive. There are no words for such a thing in my culture. In my world, all things are alive.

I've kept my distance through pure force of will. Every morning I wake with him wrapped around me, his arousal pressing into my back.

Every day I burn for him. Now, I can no longer resist. Not when these last few moments are all we have left. I press my hips back and meet his groin.

He steps closer, hand stroking my back. A question.

In answer, I reach for his hand, placing it over my breast.

If he's surprised, it's fleeting. Then he's kissing my neck, his front pressed against my back, hungry fingers stroking beneath my top.

"Sess-sha?"

My throat is so tight I can hardly speak.

His breath is hot on my skin as he plays with my breasts, teasing my nipples into tight peaks. "Tell me what you want." His deep voice hits me between my legs where I'm wet and aching for him.

"I need you. Inside me." For the first and only time.

He pushes my top down, exposing my breasts. His caresses are urgent, as if he's as desperate for this as I am.

The heavy weight of his erection presses against my behind.

He tries to turn me to face him, but I can't let him see me. My eyes are already filling with tears.

"No. Like this." I brace my hands against the rock in front of me and bend from the waist.

His large hand slides beneath my lap-lap, stroking my aching flesh. I widen my stance, desperate for his touch.

"Could you get pregnant?"

"No. I take the tamber root. It stops conception."

He continues to stroke me until I come apart against his fingers. But I need more. "Please, Malachai."

He flips up my lap-lap and strokes me some more, sliding his fingers inside me. I need him so badly I can't stand it. Not when this and the last few weeks is all I'll have to remember him by. "Fill me."

Finally, he slides the head of his cock against my sensitised flesh, and I moan. He uses it to pleasure me for a moment, then nudges my entrance, sliding into me with a long, slow glide.

He pauses, letting me adjust to his size, kissing my neck and whispering "Sess-sha, oh Sess-sha," until I want to cry.

I blink the tears back. There'll be time for them once he's gone. Right now, I want this moment with him.

He starts to love me with long smooth strokes.

I twist my head towards him, and his lips meet mine in a hungry, ravishing kiss.

"I love you." His words steal my breath.

"I love you, too."

He pumps faster, his fingers stroking between my legs just where I need them. Connection and pleasure entwine. I'm lost in him. He's everything I've ever wanted.

"*Malachai.*"

"I've got you."

His husky words are a promise.

He strokes me inside and out, faster and harder, hitting that secret spot inside me again and again until I tremble violently. I try to hold back because once it's over, *we'll* be over. But the pleasure is fierce and relentless, lifting me higher and higher.

Burning hotter and brighter.

"*Fuck, yes, Sess-sha.* Come with me."

Malachai's rough, desperate words push me over the edge. My eyes roll back in my head as I explode with a loud cry, shattering into a million pieces. His strong arm around my waist keeps me from collapsing as I clench around him. He roars, thrusting deep, clutching me tightly as I milk him of every last drop of pleasure and he spills inside me.

Our gasping breaths echo against the rocks. Noises from his people's machines filter through my pleasure haze as they prepare to leave my planet.

Watching him fly away into the stars will be unbearable. A sob bursts from my lips.

He freezes, then eases out of me, turning me to face him. "Did I hurt you?"

I shake my head.

Sitting against the rock, he cradles me in his arms, brow etched with concern. "What's wrong?"

I don't want to lose you. I cry harder.

His voice is gentle. "You're scaring me."

"You have to go." I gulp. "They're leaving. If you don't go now, you'll never be able to get home. To your people. Your planet."

"Wait. What we just did. Was that goodbye to you?"

I nod, tears coursing down my cheeks.

He frowns.

"Did you want it to be goodbye?"

"*No.*"

Cupping my face, he holds my gaze, serious. "Is this why you pulled back, why we haven't... since that first time? Because you thought I was going to leave?"

I nod.

He sighs. Then kisses my cheeks, my forehead, my nose and finally my lips. "*Oh Sess-sha.*" The words are a low growl, choked with emotion.

Dark eyes stare deep into mine and I'm almost overwhelmed by the connection.

"*Masai mendurak.*"

"What does that mean?"

"Twin soul."

"Like soul mate?"

"Yes."

"I'm your twin soul yet you would let me go?"

"There should always be choice. I would never take that away."

"Then I choose you. Always." His arms tighten around me. "You're the best thing that's ever happened to me. I don't want to go back. I want to stay here with you. If you'll have me?"

I stroke his cheek. "There's nothing I want more."

"You're my home now." He leans in and kisses me softly.

"You are my home, too."

We rest our foreheads together as it sinks in that he's staying. He's mine. Forever.

He kisses me deeply until I'm breathless.

I pull back to look into his soft eyes. "What now?"

His eyes heat. "I'm not happy that the first time I was inside you was goodbye, so now I'm going to show you how I say hello." His voice lowers and I tingle all over. "Very..." He punctuates his words with a lingering kiss. "Very..." Another kiss. "Slowly."

7
TICK TOCK
FIONA M MARSDEN

A nnie could hear nothing beyond the room, see little within. The bedchamber was in the old wing, far away from the busy parts of the house, the doors and windows heavily swathed with rich emerald velvet. The gas jet on the wall sconce was turned low as always, the cold light barely permeating beneath the canopy of the oak four-poster bed.

The new part of the house was full of Nile crocodiles and Egyptian sphinxes. Even those were long out of style, fifty years into the reign of Queen Victoria.

Annie preferred this ancient bed with its stacks of feather mattresses filling the frame which went almost as high as her waist. She was deliciously warm, burrowed under the equally prolific quilts. It hardly mattered that the fire in the grate had turned to dull coals. The current master of the house was late. Long past his usual time and she'd nodded off briefly while waiting.

The door opened with a soft click, letting in a whisper of light from the hall. A shadowed presence brought its own illumination. The glow of the candle gleamed on the brass holder and caught the gold of a sturdy old-fashioned pocket watch in a gloved hand. Annie's heart picked up the tick tock rhythm and she shifted in the bed, the better to see him.

His eyes were a brilliant silver, burned to liquid heat by the bright flame as he raised the candle and blew softly. It flickered and went out, extinguishing eyes, face and a glimpse of pale skin framed by long dark locks.

She blinked against the Stygian gloom, allowing her eyes to adjust.

Another flare of light came from the fireplace, with the rattle of coal being tipped onto the embers and stirred up with a poker. Her job, but she wouldn't complain. She could see him clearly now, the firelight reflecting off mirrors and glinting among the metal of candlesticks and adding strength to the puny gas flames.

"Are you awake?"

"No."

His chuckle warmed her. He was not inclined to levity. It was her aim to force him to smile at least once in a day. Sometimes she succeeded. More often she was rewarded with a stare and raised brows. She sat up, all the better to beat down the feathers and to see what was keeping him away. He stood very still, looking into the fire.

A shiver had her snuggling into the bedding, but it wasn't from the chill air. The fire was already sending heat into the room. "Aren't you coming to bed?"

He turned, shrugging off his coat. "I was following up on a theory. I wanted to get it written down."

His crisp vowels were a stark contrast to her words. She spoke well enough now, whipped into obedience by Cook when she'd first arrived. Later, she was motivated by her friendship with a son of the house, but it took an effort to get those plummy tones and most of the time she couldn't be bothered. He never noticed. Or at least he never commented. She wasn't sure what that indifference implied.

"Were you nervous? Anxious?"

Anxious a little. Nervous? "No. Why would I be?" It had been ten years or more since Annie had any cause for nervousness in the bedchamber. Being bedded by the youngest of the men of the household had been awkward and messy, but they'd both lacked experience. The situation now was far different. She'd been Julian Malling's mistress for years. A secret mistress in deference to her position in the house, but he came to her bed like clockwork, every month. One night only. Another one of his theories to ensure she didn't quicken with a child.

He perched on the edge of the bed and reached to tuck one of her curls behind her ear. "You look like an infant, rosy from sleep. Perhaps I shouldn't have come."

"I'm well awake now. I'll not go back to sleep." The words tumbled out before she thought better of it. If he walked away, he'd not come to her bed until the next time she finished her courses.

The momentary lightness had gone, a furrow in his brow. "I should walk away. This... arrangement... cannot remain in place forever."

Her heart thumped out its denial. "It's not harming any others. You're not wedded."

His hesitation brought her a tightness at the back of her throat.

"You're right, I'm not committed elsewhere."

"Is it likely to change?" She had no right to ask the question. It wasn't her place.

The long, beautifully defined fingers on his ungloved hand clenched. "Anything could happen."

Annie had a bad feeling about where this was going. She didn't want to know, not now. What she wanted was Julian in her bed, making love to her. Letting her love him in the only way he would allow.

"Come to bed, you'll be chilled sitting there in your shirtsleeves."

He sat for a moment, head bowed, his eyes shadowed from the light and the long wavy hair falling around his face. It was impossible to read his expression.

"If you're sure, Annie May?"

"I'm sure." She folded back the quilts in open invitation and his eyes shifted to take in the long length of her bare hip and thigh, gleaming in the dimness.

He undid his waistcoat buttons one handed and Annie slid across to reach under the waistcoat and release the braces and unbutton the trousers. His gloved hand loosely cupped her breast and she smiled up at him, still a little unnerved by his sombre expression.

"You'll find it hard to convince me you're not ready for a little pleasure, m'lord." To prove her point, she ran the back of her knuckles up the hard ridge contained by his linen drawers.

He hissed out a breath but didn't move away. "Hard is perhaps the right word for this moment."

Her own breathing eased, and her awareness of the constant tick tock increased. She glanced over at the discarded watch. It must be late, but she wasn't tired. Not with bare masculine flesh exposed to her hungry gaze.

"Take off the shirt."

He rarely did so, but after a moment where their eyes locked, he ceded her this one privilege. His easy acquiescence only increased the dread in her belly. He hated the scars from the accident, but after all these years, Annie wanted only to touch his skin. All of it, smooth or marred. She counted his youthful vanity at nought when he was barely at his majority. He was a different man now.

CR&O

Julian couldn't resist the appeal in Annie's eyes. He never could. This dependence he had on her was disturbing but as she said, it harmed no others. He remained uncertain that in some way, she was harmed by their association. There hadn't been a time in his life when Annie hadn't been there, somewhere in the background of his childhood recollections. If she wanted his shirt off, well the room was dark enough not to show the deformities he was still learning to live with. Thanks largely to Annie.

He knew her advent into his life had come when they were both not quite seven, but he'd been fascinated by her from the moment he caught her emptying the ashes in the nursery when the usual nursery maid had been off with a toothache. The bucket had been almost as large as the small, determined girl. Somehow, life before Annie had never had the same savour.

They'd had such fun when she'd been able to sneak away from her duties in the kitchen, playing hide and seek in the narrow back passages of the old house. Her sharp intelligence shocked and enthralled the boy he'd been.

The connection had been lost when he'd left for Eton, coming back for the holidays all grown up, as he'd thought, and disdaining to acknowledge the existence of a mere servant. A female at that.

He shook his head. Thinking about how things had changed later churned his stomach, raising bile at the back of his throat. Far better to focus on the pearly sheen of her skin and the pretty pink tips of her breasts in the here and now, her lovely mouth hovering close to his excitable cock.

There was a wicked glint in her eyes as she took him in hand, wrapping those capable fingers around the base, her tongue darting out to lick her lips. Not ladylike those work roughened palms, but what she did to him didn't need smooth ladylike touches.

A groan started in his gut and rattled his teeth the moment her mouth contacted his shaft. A dainty dab of her tongue made him twitch but it was the flat of it in a long stroke that sent a wobble to his knees. He braced himself with a hand on her shoulder, using the other to fondle the sensitive part of her ear. She was licking him like an Italian ice and heat tumbled through him like a burning coal down a chute, leading to an inevitable conflagration.

He jerked as his balls tightened and she gripped him harder, swallowing him to the root as he pumped into her lush mouth. She was generous to a fault, his Annie.

With legs turned to a jelly, he flopped beside her on the bed, conscious of the triumph in her bright eyes and satisfied smirk on her glossy lips.

"You want me on my knees, helpless, don't you, my Annie May?"

She shifted to allow him to roll onto the bed. "It's an option I'm considering."

"Consideration will have to wait. You've wiped me out."

"Getting old, my lord?"

He tugged her to rest her head on his right side, his stronger side. "Tired. I've not been sleeping well these nights."

She rested her hand on the scarring on his chest. "Then sleep. There's still an hour or two beyond midnight. I'll have you refreshed before we enter into more avenues of pleasure."

CƷᏰꙦ

Annie woke to the tick tock she'd become inured to in this house of mechanical marvels. Julian's workshop housed numerous small items he tinkered with during his days. Since the accident, he had become even more focussed on intellectual pursuits. He'd been unable to do more active tasks for many months. She slithered from the bed and carefully added more coal to the fire. He'd want to be unhampered by heavy quilts when he awoke.

The watch lured her with its sullen gleam. Well past midnight but hours before dawn in midwinter.

"Annie? Is everything all right?"

"I was stoking the fire. I didn't mean to disturb you."

"You know I'm very willing to be disturbed."

"Are you?"

A sharp intake of breath told her he'd heard the doubt in her voice. "For tonight anyway. Tomorrow we need to talk."

"Why not now?" She tucked herself in beside him.

"Because if we talk now, I'll not be able to pleasure you the way you want."

"Is it so bad, what we must discuss?"

His fingers trailed over her upper arm, teasing at the sensitive spot inside her elbow. "It means change, and you know I don't like change."

"True enough." She didn't like change either. It seemed she wasn't going to have any choice.

These moments when he was wholly hers in the intimacy of the night were few enough. She would take all of him whenever possible. She'd been mighty forward when he'd declared he'd not marry because of his injuries. Not wanting him to seek out a mistress, she'd gathered her courage and offered herself. It came with his rules, but the pleasures were great indeed.

He shifted over her, bracing himself with the mechanical arm he'd designed himself. It lacked the delicacy of touch he wanted but Annie was content with his use. He was an inventive lover. Tonight, she wanted only to feel the oneness with him her heart desired.

She parted her legs in invitation and he almost smiled. "Temptress."

His long fingers traced the curves of her body, tantalising her nipples, circling the hollow of her stomach until reaching their destination. She thrust her hips upward and he delved deep, his thumb brushing the little nub that held exquisite sensation.

"You're wet for me."

"Want you. Inside."

His mouth followed the trail left by his fingers and she squirmed, seeking more.

"Patience, sweetness."

His tongue was wet and warm but the moment he moved on the chill air cooled her heated skin. It was an odd feeling, confusing her senses. Forgotten at once when his mouth found the inner folds of her womanhood. A flush of heat dewed her skin as she strained up into his mouth, bracing her feet on the bed. His tongue lapped at her, tickling her bud, the heat spreading along her folds and triggering an ache deep inside.

"Please. Please. Julian." Her words blurred into babble as her insides tightened. With his seeming innate knowledge, he plunged one — no — two fingers into her sheath and she bucked against him. She dragged a quilt over her face to muffle her screams as he sent her soaring. A flight beyond stars and worlds yet not far enough, for earth beckoned too soon.

Julian rested his face on her belly, conserving his energy. It pleased him that he could give her release. She'd done everything for him. It helped to feel he was making up for the past, however meagre his efforts.

Back when they'd been sixteen, she'd seemed content enough, looking up at him with those hopeful eyes. It had been her eyes that had made him cruel after the event.

It had been his first fumbling attempt and she'd had little enough pleasure. Her whole aim had been to please him, and he'd realised it much too late. He'd been uncomfortable about what he'd asked of her immediately, questioning his motives. Shame had made him sullen.

In those long months of recuperation years later, nursed by the girl he'd wronged, he'd had far too much time to think. For all she'd appeared willing at the time, he'd been in the position of power. She'd known he could have her cast out, or at the very least, make her life a misery. Would she have made the same choice if they'd met on common ground? It had tortured him for years. Even now he knew Annie deserved more than this half-life with him.

When she'd come to him with her proposition, his first instinct, going against his body's immediate response, was to deny her. Curiosity had overwhelmed common sense and he'd asked why.

"I choose this. If you seek a mistress, I'm wishful to take the position."

"Like you chose me to take your innocence all those years ago."

"I'm not sure who was taking whose. If I recall you weren't exactly an expert." He'd had to acknowledge the hit.

"What of your work?"

"I'll not give it up. I don't want the rest of the servants to know."

So, he'd given in to his base desires. He'd placed limitations, more to protect himself than her. He'd come to need her too much. His heart was her creation and she owned it.

Annie shifted under him, her legs twining around his body. "Are you thinking hard?"

He pushed away the dark thoughts. "I'm thinking and I'm hard."

Her mouth beckoned and he fell into it, tasting her sweetness while her legs wrapped him around, bringing him closer to her. He pushed in, eased by her liquid heat. It was a coming home, a place where his damaged body became complete, transcending his limitations. The rhythm set with a tick tock that echoed in his heart as he thrust deeper, harder, seeking and finding that destination where both were one and heightened sensation became the fusing between molten bodies and souls entwined, forged together. What the gods have put together, let no man pull asunder.

ഗ൫ഋ

"A cup of tea and a boiled egg with toast for your breakfast."

Julian pushed himself into a sitting position. He'd fallen asleep in his workshop wearing his shirt and naught else. As well it was Annie and not one of the servants. "You don't have to do this, Annie. There are maids for this work."

She lay the tray on the small table he'd been using for his papers. Her neat blue gown and apron were practical, yet he found it alluring. The contrast between the lush lover of the night with her brisk efficiency in daylight.

"I don't want them coming in here and moving things. Some of the machines are delicate and they might put them out of alignment if they poke at them."

He glanced around the spacious old room, at the tables cluttered with papers and half-finished projects. The bookshelves were crammed with medical and scientific tomes. Brass and steel instruments and parts for their creations jostled with mechanical toys on the shelves. Machines sat abandoned with pipes and tubes in complicated array. Plans were pinned to walls where family portraits had once hung. "Not all the servants are as curious as you are."

"Eat your food. We have work to complete this morning."

She went to the bench she preferred and pulled a mechanism out of a tub.

He hesitated as he reached for the toast. "Have you eaten?"

Her attention was on the complexity of the contraption she was working on. "I had a slice of toast while Cook was preparing yours."

Taking a bite, he shifted a couple of papers away from the danger of egg-yolk. "What are you doing?"

"I had some ideas about increasing the tolerances. It would be better if we could attach it to a battery, but the weights are working well. As long as you keep moving, the clock is self-winding."

"What about when I'm asleep?"

She snorted. "Have you any idea how restless you are in bed? I don't think it's a problem."

He didn't think so either. "I don't fancy carrying a battery around all day and night."

Her face expressed her disdain, her lips pursed. "We've already dismissed that option. It might be a useful option for further study. If a battery could be smaller. Even the size of your palm, I can think of multiple uses."

"Maybe you could get a degree in engineering and specialise in miniaturisation. You have a gift for it." He loved her in work mode. She was always focussed. He dithered around, tempted by new ideas. She kept him on track.

Now she laughed. "If wishes were horses... I'm content here. I feel I'm accomplishing something. I don't need to go elsewhere."

"Consider the resources, the other great minds you could interact with."

She turned to face him, as if considering the idea. "What would happen to you if I weren't here? Unless you mean me to study here in London. I don't see the point."

He pushed the congealed egg and toast aside. "This isn't about me. It's about your future. It shouldn't be bound by these walls and my needs."

"You don't need me anymore? Is that what you're trying to say? Or are you talking about marriage after all. Your mother would be pleased but a wife wouldn't want me around."

Julian touched his chest. "You know I can never marry in society. Especially if I don't have you to tinker in my chest regularly."

"You know you'll be dead sooner rather than later without me here. Why push me away?"

He watched her close the small clockwork machine and place it in a China dish and uncork a bottle of pure alcohol she sloshed over the mechanism.

"I would have died years ago without your help. You shouldn't be forced to stay here, simply to keep me alive."

She was bathing her hands in the alcohol, a crease in her brows. "Why now?"

"Before it's too late for you. You've lived most of your life under this roof, subject to the whims of the master of the house. Because it's been me the last few years, doesn't give me leave to presume on your good will."

"Remove your shirt and lie down. And shift that table out of my way." She slanted a look at him. "Do you really think you're the master of this situation? I could have left any time in those twenty years. I chose to stay. I choose to be here."

He lay prone on the divan while she spread a clean sheet over his torso. He couldn't let it go. "I don't understand why you stay. There are new opportunities for women. This isn't the dark ages. Women have businesses, careers, opportunities they didn't have even a hundred years ago."

"A woman on the throne doesn't mean all women are equal. I'm still a guttersnipe, for all my education."

"Your skills rival that of a surgeon and an engineer. That makes you cleverer than both."

"Lie still and close your trap. I need a steady hand for this, or you'll not see another dawn. If I keep you alive long enough, you might even see a woman like me get to vote."

He closed his mouth and his eyes. This was the part he hated, while she removed the old mechanism and replaced it with the new. Cool fingers slid into the wound in his chest she'd mended all those years ago. The explosion of his device had broken ribs and damaged an already weak heart, the legacy that had seen him lose both father and brothers in a few short years.

Annie had been the only one willing to nurse him, the others all horrified by the damage, by the surety that he would die. She'd not only kept him alive, but she'd studied his diagrams and plans, bringing the machine in his chest to reality. Sitting beside him on those long nights when he'd hovered on the brink of death she'd studied the medical texts, using the Greek and Latin he'd taught her as a boy, secure in his superiority.

When she considered him strong enough, she'd asked him a simple question. "When do you want to die?" The choices she gave him were not hard. Risk death now, with a miniscule chance of more life, or no risk and not very much life. He'd chosen the chance she'd offered of more. Death itself did not frighten him. A lingering death was terrifying.

There was a moment after she removed the mechanism when he was certain he couldn't breathe. Then a pressure in his chest above the machine that was his heart and that first tick tock that set the pump working again, sending blood into his organs, bringing him back to life.

He opened his eyes to find her hovering, her brows drawn together. "All right?"

Nodding, he pushed back the sheet and grabbed for his shirt. When he was fully dressed, he felt able to confront her again. He pulled her to sit beside him on the divan. "Why do you stay?"

ೞ

Annie looked at Julian, so handsome, so flawed. She clasped her hands together over her aching chest as if that would ease the pain. "I love you. I've always loved you, from when you were a lad."

"I knew you were inclined to think me handsome, but surely when I took advantage of you at sixteen that changed. You couldn't love the boy I was then."

"You changed. It was bad enough when you came down from Eton the first time and you dismissed me as a mere servant. After all our friendship. Later, when we... we had congress, I thought we were mending our friendship. Yet afterward you despised me. When I walked into a room, you left. If you couldn't leave, you ignored me. Treated me as dust beneath your feet."

"No, it was never that way. It was me I despised. I used you like a trollop."

"What would you know of trollops? They're hard-working women making the best of their lives, usually after some man ruined them or through poverty. Sometimes both."

He sighed. "You're right, I know nothing of trollops, only the hard things said of them by men who use them and think nothing of it."

"It could have been me. If your father had found out, I would have been thrown into the street. What household would take me in, knowing I was easy game for the men of the house?"

"You weren't easy. I played on our affection from when we were children. For the simple reason I wanted something to boast of when I returned to Eton."

"Did you boast?"

Colour accentuated the high cheekbones. "Not a chance. By the time I returned to my schoolmates, I was too ashamed to speak of it."

"Rightly so. Yet you never came to me to apologise. Not until you lay on your deathbed. Never explained to me. I thought, once upon a time, that we were friends. Did I not deserve to be spoken to?"

"I was ashamed, yes. But I was too proud to admit it, even to you."

"Yet here we are. You deciding to send me away without explaining why. I'm not a fool. I understand the Queen's English well enough."

"You're certainly no fool, and that's the point. You could be doing much more with your life. You could train as a doctor, an engineer."

"As if they would allow someone like me in their universities. Even if I did, after all that study they wouldn't give me the same honours as a man in order to set up as a proper doctor. A surgeon in their hospitals."

"You could travel to the continent or the Americas."

Her heart tightened in her chest. "Far away. You would send me to a distant place, knowing you might not live long enough for me to see you again. Do you care so little?"

"It's because I care. You've spent years here as a servant, doing things no servant would do."

"I chose to take you to my bed. It was my choice."

His laugh came out strangled. "I'm not talking of bedding you. I'm talking of all you do here, for me in my... our... laboratory. I couldn't have achieved anything without you. I wouldn't be alive without you. Isn't it time you had a life of your own?"

"A life I choose? This is what you are sending me away for? To live the life I choose. You are such a... *a man*. And I don't mean in a good way."

"You're accusing me of not talking to you, not asking you. I plead guilty. Perhaps I don't want to ask you. Of all the things I fear, it is of you walking away. If I send you, at least I have not kept you from selfishness. I have not succumbed to my need, my fear."

His lip quivered. "Most of all I fear asking you and having you stay. Because if you choose to stay now, I could never let you go and I think the world will be a lesser place. You could accomplish so much good in the world, as you've done for me."

She spread her arms. "Look at all the things we do together. The designs you send to manufacturers to improve their machines. To make them safer for the workers; for those who use the machines. Is that not enough?"

"Here we are tied together, I don't want to be the one to hold you back."

"Hold me back? Julian Malling, it is you who gave me wings. You taught me to read, you allowed me to work with you in your workshop, to learn from your books, from watching you work. From working side by side with you. Everything I am came because of those gifts you gave me."

"You are far more than what you can do. It is your heart and mind that takes those small gifts and turns them into remarkable things. I tried for years to bring my ideas to fruition. Your skills make them real. Practical."

"No one else would have given me the opportunity. I will always be grateful for it."

"I don't want gratitude."

"It is not a sin to feel gratitude. It is not gratitude that created the love I feel for you in my heart. It is knowing you, all you have been, good and bad, all you could be. That is why I love you. It isn't conditional on my place here. You could send me to the ends of the earth, and I would still love you, and ache for you."

He reached for her wrist, drawing her closer. "Do you ache for me?"

"Every moment." His heat touched her even at this distance. "Loving you means wanting you, in all ways. With my mind, my heart, my soul." She flattened one hand against his chest. "With my body, I thee worship."

Dragging her close, he pressed her against his body. His lips dragged along her throat, seeking out her pulse. "I have loved you since before I knew there was such a thing. I fought against it when I realised it wasn't acceptable to my peers. It made me angry, and anger made me clumsy. I could not believe in a second chance and held you at a distance, even as I relied on you for every beat of my heart, every breath."

Annie squirmed in his grip, seeking out his mouth. She wanted him with the essence of all she was. "No more words."

His eyes burned down at her. "You'll marry me, my other half, my soul?"

"There's no need."

"There is. I want no more secrecy. I want to show you off, as my partner, my friend, and my lover." He moved her hand to rest over the machine in his chest. It resounded with a steady tick tock beat under her fingers. "Giver of life, maker of hearts. My heart."

8

HARVESTING LOVE

JENNIFER WESTGARTH

"For fuck's sake, Sam. When the hell are the parts arriving for the harvester? You said they'd be here Monday. It's now Friday and I don't have a fucking working machine."

And just like that, my day turns to shit.

If she wasn't my boss's daughter, I'd tell Andi where to stick her goddamn attitude about things that are out of my control. But since her dad became ill a few months back, she's stepped up, and worked just as hard as everyone else. Even if some days, she takes the term taskmaster way too seriously.

But I love my job. So instead, I do what I've become a freaking master at recently, and take a calming breath, counting to five before sliding out from under the tractor and standing to face her.

She's a foot shorter than me, but what she lacks in height she makes up for in venom. And for that, she has my complete respect. Even if I don't always show it.

"Well?" Her eyebrows shoot up and she shoves a dirty hand in my direction as if I'm going to place the parts in it.

"I'm not a magician, Andi." I pull the rag from the waistband of my jeans and wipe as much excess oil from my hands as I can. "And as shitty luck would have it, I don't control the suppliers, the delivery runs, or the weather."

"We can't harvest if we don't have a working harvester, Sam."

I touch my fingers to my chest and gasp. "Oh, is that how it happens? The machine has to... work?"

That earns me a major eye roll and a huff that could blow out a bonfire. "Don't be an arsehole. We need to get this crop off before the weather turns and the seed gets downgraded. Or, worse, we lose it completely. We've been working day and night for weeks, and I will *not* let everything get fucked up because we can't finish the last paddock."

She turns to storm out of my office — yes, that's what I call the machinery shed because it's where I do my best work — but I catch her wrist in my hand before she can disappear.

"Andi."

She stops with her back to me and barely turns her head.

We could battle all day with our razor-sharp tongues, but she needs to know I'm serious when it comes to this property. So I forgo the smartarse comments for a moment and lower my voice.

"Hey, I'm not out here doing nothing all day while your dad lies in hospital getting worse. I realise how important it is for him to know the farm will be looked after when he's gone. I treat it like it's my own and I'm doing everything I can to get this crop off before it's too late. Don't ever doubt that."

Her shoulders drop and her head lowers, eyes trained on the ground by her feet. Her slow, deep breath tells me she's trying her best to stay calm.

"I don't doubt you, Sam. But this farm is everything to me. And if we lose the first crop Dad hasn't been a part of, it'll haunt me forever. I have to—"

My phone ringing cuts her off, *Rocketman* blasting from its speakers. I ignore it. She clearly needs to say what's on her mind.

"You going to get that?"

"No."

The music plays for another moment before she whips around to face me, throwing her hand up to her temple. "Argh! I hate that song. Will you *please* make it stop?"

I swipe my phone off the workbench and hit the green answer button out of habit. Damn it.

"Sam Franklin," I say, putting it to my ear.

Andi looks around the shed while she waits, her eyes scanning the ride-on mower, chisel plough, forklift, harrow, some irrigation equipment, and the tractor I was working on when she blew in here like a storm that would destroy the crops.

"Yep... Got it... Thanks. Tomorrow morning... Yeah, first thing. See you then."

I hang up and return my phone to the workbench.

Andi doesn't wait for an invitation to continue. She doesn't need one. "I'm going to see Dad tomorrow. I need to tell him everything's fine, Sam, and I can't lie to him."

"You don't have to lie, because everything *will* be fine."

She chuckles softly and leans against the tractor, folding her arms over her chest. "Optimism in the face of disaster. I'm not sure whether that's admirable or just plain stupid."

"Neither. That was Joe," I tell her. "The parts are in."

ဢજ૦

The son of one of Dad's old high school buddies, Sam's worked here for the last decade, starting out with odd jobs around the place, all gangly limbs, greasy hair and an awkward smile. I'd seen him as a sort of half-brother, or second cousin twice removed. Someone I had to get to know but didn't take any notice of.

That is until he grew into his six-foot frame and developed pecs and an eight pack.

More importantly, he started looking like he really belonged here. As though he's meant for this place. Like me.

I first dreamt about him a year ago. I woke up in the middle of the night, sweaty, breathless, and *wet*. I'd never had a sex dream before, and damn if I didn't try falling back to sleep so I could have another one. Ever since, I've replayed the moment from my dream, when Sam took me in the machinery shed and made my world tilt off its axis with his touch; his hands familiar with every curve of my body, his fingertips finding my most sensitive nerves under my summer dress. Side note – I knew it was a dream as I never wear dresses. But, Holy Christ, he set my body on fire in that shed and I've been using the dream as inspiration whenever I feel lonely in bed at night. Or in the morning. And a few times in the middle of the day. And once on the harvester.

As the only female on the farm, I've had to keep my guard up. I've made it my mission to learn to do everything the guys do, and developed my language to suit. No precious girly constitution to offend here. I didn't want to be seen as different. I always knew that one day, as an only child, I was going to inherit the farm, and no-one was going to tell me I was unsuitable when the time came.

Only, that time is much closer than any of us anticipated.

It's time to admit what I'm sure Dad's known all along; Sam is as dedicated to this place as I am. Maybe I don't have to do it all on my own.

When he finally gets out to his truck, I'm leaning against the bull bar with toasted sandwiches wrapped in baking paper and two travel mugs of coffee.

"Figured you wouldn't have had breakfast yet," I say, pushing off the vehicle and heading to the passenger door.

"How early did you get up?" Sam unlocks the truck and jumps up into the cab. I have to throw the sandwiches on the dash first, freeing a hand to pull myself up by the grab handle on the roof.

"Four. I knew you'd be leaving at the crack of dawn and wanted to come with you."

"Why?"

"Because I appreciate everything you've been doing lately and thought you might like some company while you drive into town."

The engine rumbles deep and low and Sam stares at me for a moment. Like he's trying to figure out what he's looking at.

"What?" I say, refusing to regret my decision not to lie in bed this morning and get lost in a book and a freshly brewed coffee in my favourite mug.

He shrugs as we start to move off, turning his eyes to the driveway and leaving the house behind us. "Just that Saturday mornings are usually yours to yourself. It's pretty much the only time you relax and get up later than five a.m."

God, he knows me too well. Almost.

The words to explain form in my head and I get ready to say them — that I want to spend time with him. Alone. That I can't stop thinking about my dream and I want to kiss him until I'm breathless and our lips hurt and I almost pass out. That I want him to touch me everywhere.

But like every other time, they get stuck in my throat and I don't say any of that. Instead I unwrap our sandwiches and hand him one, taking a sip of my coffee.

"Just felt like doing something different," is all I can manage.

We spend the rest of the drive in silence, taking in the sunrise and listening to the radio. Half an hour later we reach town and meet with Joe, who would never normally come into work this early.

"You're a superstar, Joe. We really appreciate this." Sam grabs the box of parts and we head for the door of the shop, Joe following us to lock back up.

"No trouble at all, you both know that."

Just before Joe gets the door closed, Sam turns back. "We should have you and Viv over for dinner after the crop's off. We won't have time before then, but it'd great to catch up soon. It's been too long."

We?

Sam nods at me "We could do a roast."

I stare at him, trying not to read anything into that tiny word.

"Sound great, guys. Now go to work, cause I'm going home for breakfast."

Pleasantries over, I lead the way back to Sam's truck in the quiet street.

The sun has only just hit the sky and something about the silence around us and the hope that's blooming in my chest for the day that's emerging, makes me continue our conversation from earlier.

"Why don't *you* ever relax, by the way?" I say, getting back into my seat and buckling up.

"Why don't I *what*?"

"You know, sleep in, have some time to yourself. I mean, I thought I was dedicated to the farm, but sometimes I think you work harder than I do."

He's quiet for a few moments as he shrugs out of his jacket and settles behind the wheel, then slowly turns his gaze to me.

Why is he staring at me again? He's got to stop. Surely he doesn't mean to, but he's causing my temperature to rise to unhealthy levels. And why am I holding my breath?

"Sometimes?" he finally says, with that smirk that infuriates me. It's what he does when he's about to win an argument. Well, not this time.

I disguise the release of my breath with a loud "Ha!" and call him on his accusation.

"If you think you put more effort than I do into that place, you're so far off base you're not even playing the same game. The *tiny* amount of time I allow myself to recharge my batteries, I can't even manage to switch off my brain. I'm still figuring out costs and purchasing and—"

Suddenly, Sam's lips are on mine.

Woah... what the hell is happening? Am I dreaming again?

His hand is at the back of my head and his tongue swipes my top lip.

But then... nothing.

I open my eyes to see him sitting back in his seat, panting.

"Shit. Christ, Andi, I'm so sorry. I shouldn't have done that. I didn't even ask. I'm *so* sorry." He runs a hand through his thick hair and anguish crosses his face. "Are you okay? Please don't slap me." How can he sound so sexy when he's apologising? "Or punch me in the balls. Although I deserve it. But I'd prefer it if you didn't. God, I'm—"

Without thinking, I unbuckle my seat belt like it's on fire and launch myself at him, kissing him hard and not at all sophisticated.

I open my mouth for him and he accepts my offer immediately, claiming my tongue and my mind at the same time.

We're frantic for a moment, hands rushing over each other's bodies, grabbing fistfuls of clothing as if we're not parked in the middle of the main road in town which will soon be buzzing with morning traffic.

Then Sam's hands are on my cheeks, pulling me back from his face only long enough for both of us to take a breath, and for him to attempt a question I'm not ready to answer.

"What are we—"

I kiss him again, this time a little slower, as I climb over the centre console and straddle his strong thighs. The groan that starts from deep within his chest encourages me, as do his massive hands as they cup my arse and squeeze.

Everything around me falls away except Sam. Nothing exists except this moment. I try not to grind myself on him, worried I'll crush what I can feel through my cargos is clearly *very* interested in what's going on here. But my body is reacting to Sam like it has to no other man and my hips roll forward, backward, forward, without my permission.

Heat spreads through my core and my head falls back as a moan escapes me. Sam latches onto my neck, digging his tongue into my pulse point, setting off sparks behind my eyes and in between my legs. Shamelessly, I grind against his hard-on and Sam raises his hips once, twice, three times, showing me what he'd be doing if there were no clothes separating our flesh.

Suddenly, he grabs my hips with strong fingers, preventing them from moving.

"Oh my God, Andi. We've got to stop."

"No, please," I beg him.

"We have to. We're in the main street, anyone could see us."

I open my eyes and reality comes back into view. Peering through the back windows of the truck, I see lights flickering on in nearby shops. "Fuck."

Sam laughs and kisses my chin, pushing hair from my face.

"Almost."

ᏨᏋᎪᏓ

Dinner that evening is a barbeque with everyone on the back deck and a carton of ice-cold beer. With everything going according to plan for the rest of the day, the tension visibly rolls off Andi's shoulders as she finishes her drink, and excuses herself for the evening.

My dick twitches as she turns to glance at me on her way to the house, and I've never wanted anything more desperately than to follow her right now. But I know if I stand, my jeans will look like they're hiding a divining rod and Andi is the only water for miles.

So I hold my ground; I don't want to give anyone a reason to suspect something is going on between us. Because I have no idea how to explain what happened in the cab of my Ute this morning.

An hour later, the boys have gone for the day and I'm back in my office, packing away tools I used to fix the harvester this morning and tidying up my work benches — I like to actually be able to find shit when I need it.

Outside, the evening breeze whistles around the building but, unlike any other night, there's a scent in the air I can't place. Something fruity, maybe flowers. I breathe in deep, lifting my head to follow it. It's earthy, too. Like fresh cut grass or hay bales. Sandalwood?

"Thought we could indulge in a glass of the good stuff."

I turn to see Andi leaning against the frame of the shed, holding a bottle of The Macallan and two glasses. It's her dad's favourite scotch and it only gets brought out for celebrations. But the bottle in her hand is not what's got me tongue tied - unable to put a mature sentence together in my head, let alone speak aloud.

Andi. Is. Wearing. A. Dress.

It's light, flowy, stops at her knees, and shows a hint of cleavage that I want to lick The Macallan from.

Holy shit.

As she comes closer, the scent becomes stronger and I assume it's her shampoo or body wash or something. Images of pressing her up against the tiles in the shower flash in front of my eyes and I hope like hell she's been having similar thoughts. Why else would she come out to the machinery shed looking nothing like I've ever seen before?

I could assume she's going into town for a while. Maybe to the pub to dance with her friends and let off some steam. But even the few times a year she does that, Andi only ever swaps her work jeans for her *good* jeans. She's never gone out looking like this.

Finally, I manage actual words.

"What are we celebrating?"

Andi smiles and it's a picture I wish I could hang on the wall of the shed, to look at every day.

"We did it. We got the first crop off without Dad. Not that that's something I wish we were celebrating but, nonetheless, I'm grateful. To everyone." She pours three fingers of scotch into each glass and hands me one, not letting it go when I close my fingers around the low ball.

"Especially you," she says, letting her fingers slip from my glass as she takes a mouthful from hers.

I do the same, and we stand for a moment, letting the silence do its job and push us together. Andi moves first, closing the gap between us with one last step and rising onto her toes. Her gaze drops to my mouth, but when she leans in, she doesn't kiss me. Instead, her soft lips graze my neck, her breath fanning my skin, bringing goosebumps out everywhere and making my toes dig into my boots.

"I want to kiss you," she whispers just below my ear.

My eyes close and thoughts of the things I want to do her make my breath quicken.

"Then kiss me."

I turn my head so she catches my lips with hers and let her set the pace. It's slower than in the truck this morning. And I'm grateful. I almost exploded right before we stopped, and I wouldn't have been able to look her in the eye for days had that happened. Maybe weeks. But this… this is perfection.

"I want to touch you." Her voice is raspy, sexy as hell, and the desperation in it makes me harder than I thought possible.

"Then fucking touch me," I growl.

The next thing I know, Andi's hands are under my shirt, her fingers running gently over my skin as it burns for her. My breath falters as she flashes me a smile that I bet she stole from the devil.

"You said *fuck*." She raises one eyebrow. "You never say that."

"I think the situation calls for it."

She smiles again, making a start on the buttons of my shirt. She plucks the first few open and kisses my chest, pushing the fabric aside to flick her tongue over my nipple.

Oh Christ, she's incredible. She's beautiful, smells amazing, and...

"Wait, Andi..." I take a step back, remembering I haven't showered and I'm still in my work clothes from today. "I'm filthy—"

She tilts her head and traces my backward step with her forward one. "Good."

I can't help but chuckle. "Really?" Maybe one day I'll find out just how filthy she wants me to be.

Taking another mouthful of her scotch, Andi puts her glass down and reaches her hand behind my neck, gently pulling me toward her. As she kisses me, I feel the liquid trickle into my mouth, flicking every switch in my body onto full power.

I can't hold back anymore.

As I pick her up, gripping the backs of her thighs, Andi wraps her legs around me like it's a move we've practiced before. And she fits perfectly. Our mouths meet, urgent, demanding, made for each other.

Her fingers scrape my scalp as she runs them through my hair and the slight pain turns me on even more. I wonder if she likes that, too. Something to experiment with later...

I walk us to the ride-on mower and set her down on the hood of the engine. I kiss her hard, pressing myself against her centre so she can feel what she does to me.

Her long blonde hair is caught up on top of her head, exposing her neck, and this time it's my turn to feast. I felt the way she responded to my tongue in the truck this morning, so I start with the same move, and get the same result. The sound I cause her to make is like a whip to my back, spurring me on, making me go harder.

I reach between her legs and — holy shit, she's not wearing underwear.

She came here with one thing in mind tonight, and I'll be damned if I'm going to deny her what she wants. One problem...

"Andi," I can barely speak. "I don't have condoms out here."

She shakes her head, her legs bent, feet braced on the wheels below, and points to her upper arm. "Implant."

"I'm clean," I promise her. "I haven't been with anyone for—"

"Me too, but I thought you said you were filthy." She looks up at me with dark eyes and I know we're good to go.

I tease the beautiful flesh at her centre, finding her swollen clit and circling it with a gentle finger.

"Oh, God, Sam!"

I slide my hand around her neck and pull her to me. I want her lips back on mine. "Yes, beautiful?" I say into her mouth, my fingers still working her clit. I'm desperate to push inside her, but I don't. I decide in that moment I want my cock to be the first part of me she feels that way.

Her thighs tremble around my hand and her head falls back, breath quickens, eyelids flutter closed. Jesus, is she going to pass out if she comes? Or worse, before?

Suddenly, she sits up, tugs at my belt and frees it from the loops that hold it in place with a swift, bold manoeuvre. I unbutton my jeans and kick my steel caps off at the same time, while Andi works her dress up around her hips, exposing what I'm going out of my mind to feel clenched around me. After shoving my jeans down my legs and stepping out of them, I lift Andi off the hood of the mower, bringing our bare skin together for the first time. I step to the side and climb up to the seat, settling her on my lap as I sit down.

She's inches away from where I want her, and she's clearly as unhappy about it as I am.

"Sam, I need you inside me," she says on a breath, lifting herself and circling her hips with agonising precision, making my tip wet.

I raise my hips and push at her entrance, making her gasp. Then she takes over, lowering herself onto me in one go, eliciting a growl I've never heard come out of me before.

And just like that, I'm ruined for anyone else. Nothing will ever compare to this moment. Andi lifts herself again and drops down, then again, and again, and I'm about to do every man in the world an injustice by blowing my load after seven and a half seconds.

Perhaps she senses that, because she stills for a moment, her hands around my neck, and rests her forehead on mine.

"I've wanted you for so long, Sam," she says, beginning to rock ever so slightly, the same way she did to me in the truck this morning, but agonisingly slow.

I run my fingers up and down her back, then grab her arse and encourage her motion. "Why haven't you ever told me?"

Following my lead, Andi quickens her pace, grinding on my pelvis as tiny whimpers escape her. "I wasn't sure how you'd feel. Boss's daughter and all that. Didn't want the other guys to give you shit."

I drive up into her with a scowl on my face and a determination that surprises me. She's telling me we could've done this before now? "Fuck the other guys."

She manages a tiny laugh. "No thanks. Only you."

"You're goddamn right, only me. From now on, Andi. It's only me."

I reach behind her and turn the key in the ignition, bringing the machine to life under us.

The vibration thrums through my balls immediately, and Andi cries out as I thrust upwards again, and again, savouring the perfect sounds she's making. I want them as my new ringtone.

I still my hips, grabbing hers and grinding her against me to give her clit the attention it needs from this position. It works.

She's so worked up already, Andi digs her nails into my shoulders and screams.

"Yes! Sam. Oh my God! Yes!" Clenched like a vice around my cock, she comes harder than I could've imagined. I slow her hips momentarily, but don't stop, then power up for a second one. Increasing the speed again, I hope to God she's not burnt out. "Oh, Christ. I'm... again." She's not. "Fuck, yeeeees! Oh, God, Sam."

And with that, I follow, thrusting from under her, feeling my balls tighten and the veins in my neck about to pop as I come just as hard as Andi did.

I'm still shaking minutes later when I lift her head off my shoulder and kiss her jaw. Temple. Forehead.

"Let's get back to the house," I say. "I've got plans for you that involve a shower and my tongue."

"Mmmm. Sounds good," she mumbles, as we climb off the mower.

I pull my jeans on as Andi grabs The Macallan and our glasses, and we make our way back to the main house. She's a step ahead of me as we get to the veranda, and I reach out to catch her wrist like I did in the shed yesterday. This time, she turns around immediately.

I kiss her gently, wrapping an arm around her lower back. When she breaks the kiss, her smile lights up the evening sky. "A dream of mine came to life today," she says. "Is it too soon to say that I never want it to end?"

Just then, *Closing Time* by Semisonic interrupts us as my phone rings.

Andi quirks an eyebrow at me. "You going to get that?"

"No."

She grins and I let the call go through to voicemail.

As we make our way inside, she says, "You changed your ring tone. Why?"

I shrug like it's no big deal. "Someone I care about didn't like my last one. And I plan on spending a whole lot more time with her so don't want to piss her off."

As we climb the stairs to the bathroom, Andi says her last coherent words for the evening. "Smart man."

9
THE GEARS OF LOVE
KATRINA LOUISE

I've countless questions needing answers. For example, in six thousand years of civilisation, and over two centuries of industrialisation, how come we've invented pocket-sized machines more advanced than our first spacecraft, but hair conditioner still resembles male ejaculate?

Further-bloody-more, why didn't one sodding violinist care to inform me that, in my rush to make rehearsals that hair wash morning, I'd missed a conditioner splodge in my ear? A fellow cellist finally piped up, but not before the strings sniggered, '*There's something about Emelia. Wink, nudge, wink*'.

Today's curly questions out-twist my kinky hair. Why'd mum lie and dad sustain it? Am I bonkers digging up ancient history? How awkward will this get-together be?

Having checked both ears in the rear-view mirror, I open the Fiat's door and land my yellow sandals in a puddle. Flapping my feet beneath cuffed jeans flicks away summer rain. But a bigger concern than soggy sandals is my top's plunging neckline. Shite, it flaunts more skin than I thought.

The sound of a wolf whistle jerks up my chin. Bolts of heat char my cheeks as cocky Italian lads swagger down the lane. One strides backwards blowing kisses. Too much cleavage is inconceivable for the city of Roma. Reverse the Italian spelling and you get *amor*. Fun fact, Rome ranks 8th in Tinder's most active European cities. London, my hometown, polls top position.

Muttering, I lock the car. All roads lead to Rome, but navigating its frenetic streets is an exercise in self-jeopardy. Still, Aunt Zarina insisted that her limited traffic zone permit was worth it. Now we're finally parked with Zarina off shopping, it's time for me to haul arse, as Americans say. Legs pumping over cobblestones I disregard the spray. My bag strap cuts across my chest containing my heart rattling my ribs. I'm notoriously tardy, hope he doesn't think that I've stood him up.

My throat's reflexive tsk mocks, *this isn't a romantic date!* We were childhood friends. Nothing more. *Less*, in fact. Acquaintances at best. The boy I'd shared seven summers with had long grown up and beyond my reach, well before he moved to New York.

No doubt his mum commanded this outing. Thirteen years on and Sylvie is still urging her son to babysit me, just like she did when we were kids and Sylvie was a seamstress in Nonno's tailor shop.

Transcending the space-time continuum, sewing machines hum. Clackety-clack, bobbins whirr and spindles buzz. Clunk-a-clunk, needles punch. Sounds etched in my memory.

Lost in a nostalgic fog, I gasp turning the corner. He stands by a dingy motorbike. Less lanky lad, more Latin Adonis nowadays.

Raffaello Nardin. Celebrity photographer. Model dater. Friend of rockstars and indie creatives. Six-foot-one of *bella mascolinita*. Dressed in black. Olive skin. Liquorice mane styled short back and sides beneath long tussled waves. Biceps strain his t-shirt sleeves. Manly thighs fill his jeans. Hirsute, brawny forearms replace the boyish ropes I knew.

Close up he's sultry like the sky above. Chiselled jaw. Long, straight nose. Plump lips with a prominent top bow defined by dusky stubble. Ice blue eyes narrow beneath proud jet brows.

"Ciao, Emelia," he purrs with his memorable, lopsided grin.

As lips brush my cheek I revert to lovesick teen. Clackety-clack my pulse whirs and buzzes. Clunk-a-clunk my heart thuds.

Raffaello pulls back, eyes dipping to my bust.

Whoa, okay, folded arms don't help, they squeeze and hoist. A physical late bloomer, I was flat as a board our last joint summer. Think I overdid the prayers that year for bazonkers to rival Mina Scarsella's, the object of teenage Raff's affections. Wound up with 34DDs.

Sweet relief, Raff's eyes lift. The roomy swing dress I wore at grandad's funeral shrouded my curves. No longer a scrawny girl whose only asset was toffee-hued, bum-length curls, womanly hips and a buxom chest changed my fortune with the opposite sex.

But feminine endowments are a mixed blessing. Today's fast consumer society views female bodies as disposable commodities. Easy to pick up and put down again. That's why I normally keep my curves hidden in baggy tees and loose-fit jeans. Even my orchestra blacks are shapeless sacks.

Because blowed if I'll let some bloke, who craves a poke, discard me just like everyone else. I grew up disowned and adrift. Can't recall mum or life before boarding school. My childhood consisted of uneasy Easters with dad's new family and Christmas in Milan with Aunt Zarina. Roman summers skated closest to homely.

"There's still sadness in your eyes," he observes.

In fairness, things have gone to pot. I buried Nonno last week, feel guilty for letting my music ambitions curtail my Rome visits, and learned my dad is a blooming imposter. Then there's the cherry atop my shit sundae — Raff, the childhood chum who spawned my first and greatest boy crush was coerced to invite me on this pity tryst.

Still, despite underscoring my loneliness, camaraderie is sorely needed.

Clearing my throat, I downplay with a shrug. "Adulting is a grim business."

His sympathetic smile makes me sway. "Amen to that."

A symphony of sewing machines erupts in my erogenous zones. My thread tension tightens, accursed hormones.

He taps the seat of the two-wheeled contraption behind him. "Meet my Scrambler. Shall we go for a ride?"

On this junkyard rig?

Oozing masculine grace he swings a leg over, flashing Casanova-like finesse at mounting things.

"I know she doesn't look much." He tosses me a helmet. "But beauty lies in the eye of the beholder."

I'm hit with another swoony grin as he fastens his chinstrap. Raff gestures for me to sit behind. "Hold tight to me." His directive thrills and terrifies. "Let's see where life takes us."

CR80

The year he turned seventeen — our last Roman summer — Raff's skin cleared, and he grew four inches. Whereas me, Miss-Thirteen-No-Training-Bra-Needed, sprouted braces, my skin resembled pizza and my insides went squishy thinking of boys. One Italian boy in particular.

Now with arms looped around Raff's torso, my boobs are squished behind that dish and my thighs brace his hips. My footwear isn't regulation and my lack of a protective jacket problematic, yet my biggest concern is shielding my surging lady boner.

The Scrambler's motor vibrates beneath us. It's noisy and rattly like the oft-repaired, ancient sewing machines which Nonno swore superior to modern equivalents. Motorbikes don't turn me on, though wrapped around Raff I'll dismount with damp knickers even without the undercarriage massage.

Cruising by the Colosseum, the road smooths from bumpy black basalt to asphalt.

"We used to play here," he shouts.

"Don't you mean, tease gladiator touts?"

Christ, his chuckling shoulder bounce is sexy.

The Scrambler skirts Palatine Hill with a high-pitched drone. Our vista narrows to a maze of lanes, and we park in the Pantheon's shadow. Once stopped I clamber off and wrestle the jolly helmet off. We tousle our tresses in unison. With headgear slung on the handlebars and a knapsack retrieved from a scuffed saddlebag, Raff pulls out a camera.

Ambling through Piazza della Rotonda, luminous, lilliputian lagoons cover the square from residual rain. Raff examines a puddle closely. Lens aimed south he eyeballs the viewfinder and rotates the focus ring. The shutter clicks.

"Sometimes to discover real beauty, it helps to try a different angle."

Bright eyes find mine as he lowers the camera. His friendly expression entices me closer.

"Trust me, Em, you won't fall in."

Looking down, I spy a liquid portal to a capsized realm. The sky transforms to an inky ocean filled with topsy-turvy starlings. Flipped arched windows resemble horseshoes. The Pantheon's dome hovers suspended as tourists stroll upside down.

"It's a funfair mirror," I observe giddily.

"Reflection photography."

"Stunning," I gush as my stomach gurgles.

"Let's eat," he suggests with a breathy chuckle, extending an arm.

Our hands slide together effortlessly, his palm against mine.

The sun's reappearance turns rain into vapour. We visit a deli from our youth. Its scored checkerboard floor hasn't altered with time and cured meats still dangle from the ceiling. We purchase fresh focaccias stuffed with prosciutto, artichokes, olives, and bocconcini.

Perched by the fountain I tie back my hair and tuck into lunch.

"What's the story with the bike?" I ask between bites.

We fall into our established roles of Raff the raconteur and Emelia the keen listener with occasional rejoinders.

"Early last century, crazy Englishmen raced motorcycles around the countryside. They prized speed over rules and aimed to cross the finish line in record time, by any means."

"Sounds dangerous."

"When normal bikes struggled with the conditions, they modified. Boosted off-road suspension with all-terrain tyres. Ground parts off, welded bits on, anything to amplify torque."

"Torque? I know my way around an Oyster card but not much more."

Twisting sideways he places one hand on my diaphragm, another on my lower spine. "When an engine changes gear, the torque is acceleration's thrust." I lurch with his push. "The tug forcing you forward."

He lets me go. My breathing stays laboured.

"Madcap inventors who scrambled to win created Scramblers, so I make myself one."

"Like Frankenstein's monster."

"I hate our obsession with perfection. We polish flaws until character is gone and worship surface glitter. Does anyone care what's beneath the veneer? Show me the interior."

The passion which grips him suspends my breathing.

Raff shakes his head and gives a ragged sigh. "Machines fascinate me. Their elegance. Design. Functionality. Artistry. I like pulling them apart to see how they work. Toaster. Wristwatch." He jangles his. "The craftsmanship that we take for granted blows my mind. Especially when the smartest gadgets possess simplicity."

"You talk like you prefer machines to people."

He opens his mouth and takes a man-sized bite. I'm riveted by his Adam's apple when he swallows.

"My photography subjects remind me of robots."

Shifting on my tailbone I straighten my posture.

"Models are designed to pose their bodies. When they attempt conversation, things malfunction."

"I thought dating models was a fetish of yours."

Flinty eyes flick to mine. "I stopped because they don't care about me."

My heart skips a beat.

"They care about parties, things I buy, people I know. It's easy to mistake pleasure for love when you are young. I'm wiser now and I've learned the hard way — one doesn't lead to the other."

I've long admired Raff for speaking his mind, but his candour is confronting.

"Those girls don't worry if I'm sick or miss my mamma. They worship glamour and can't understand why I question their meaningless existence and yearn to photograph something other than vanity."

Filling my lungs to ease the ache, I hold my breath for a beat before letting it out.

"*Scusa*, Emelia." His knee bumps my leg. "I bring the mood down."

"Sounds like you've been soul-searching since turning thirty."

His lips creep up at the corners. "I forget how easy we talk."

"Must be my *not a supermodel* vibe." My sarcastic tone is a hostile response to my mum's past that I can't control.

"You find me easy too?"

Raff's English is usually so refined from living abroad that when he flubs his words, it emboldens me to share my secret.

ೞ

Menacing clouds suffocate the sky when Raff closes the letter that changed my life. When mum got sick, she wrote me this note and gave it to Nonno, instructing him to hold it until I was old enough to understand. I suspect a child would've coped better than an adult forced to process a lifetime of lies.

It's a sadistic fairy tale. Aren't they all?

Two sisters raised by a widowed tailor leave Rome seeking fortune and fame.

Zarina settles in Milan, working for a designer.

Felicia models fashion in London, where a whirlwind romance grants her a British husband and visa. The marriage ends around the time she falls pregnant. The baby — that would be me — ruins her career. Then, six years later, Felicia meets her maker, foisting her now half-orphaned daughter onto ex-husband Nathan, who ships the girl to boarding school and doggedly avoids her.

Scratching his jaw, Raff slumps on the plinth. "*Merda*. Nathan isn't your real papa."

"Nope." I plonk alongside him. "That honour goes to a Syrian Kurd named Daristan. Surname unknown. How *not* to fix a marriage on the rocks — have unprotected sex with a hot, exotic stranger."

"Does Nathan know?"

"He agreed to his name on my birth certificate, and I doubt he'd take custody of a kid who wasn't his. But given we look nothing alike and have never been close, I'm convinced he always suspected. No wonder he constantly palms me off — the bastard offspring of his dead ex-wife and some random in need of a condom."

Raff's eyebrows bunch tighter when emotion overcomes me. Burying my face in my palms, I sniff and shudder with a case of ugly-crying. "All my life I've felt displaced. Abandoned by mum. Forsaken by Nathan. Thinly tolerated by Zarina. Even Nonno couldn't afford my full-time upkeep."

A hand slides around my shoulder, cajoling me into a seated hug. Despite my nose being clogged with snot, the scents of bergamot and musk seduce my nostrils when I nuzzle Raff's neck.

Lips dust my hair. His palm buffs my arm. I'd gladly stay wrapped in his embrace all day, but the heavens open. Worming my face to the surface, I blink at rain splatters. The square empties and we scramble to our feet, clutching one another like buoys in a storm.

Unconcerned by getting wet, he grins and pulls me into a spin. "Remember dancing in the rain?"

Suddenly I'm eight again and he's just twelve, a golden pre-pubescent age, mimicking Hollywood musical routines adored by Sylvie.

"Life is messy!" Raff shouts above the downpour. He clasps my waist. We spontaneously sway. "And *bellissima!*"

My hands rest on his shoulders, skin tingling from the rain. Our feet slow and gazes lock, a connection as solid as his physical hold. Moisture is everywhere but my mouth. The downpour plays prestissimo, as does my heart. Raff's crotch nudges mine and the world turns diagonal as our lips drift closer.

"Sorry!" I bleat, staggering backwards.

Flirting with fantasy titillates. Reality petrifies. Tucking my chin, I'm horrified to see two obvious nubs where my nipples push against my top. Onlookers shelter beneath the Pantheon's portico. Hugging my torso, I stride, head down, towards the Scrambler.

By the time I reach the bike, the weather Gods — barbarous bastards — stop the rain. Raff approaches with a hangdog expression.

"I'll take you home," he says, his voice flat like his eyes.

Sucking back fresh tears, I can't decide if I've been dumb or wise.

ᚼᚱᛒᛞ

We pull up to Nonno's shop. It's Sylvie's now. Raff unlocks the door leading to the upstairs apartment. Nonno hasn't lived here since the nursing home. Sylvie has a flat nearby.

"Why bring me here and not my hotel?"

"To me your home is here."

While I'm silent and still, he scrubs the back of his neck. "Let me make a pot of coffee to say goodbye."

His tone's brutal finality chills my core.

"I can't dump you looking like a drowned cat," he adds.

Though he muddles the saying, the unflattering image scraps the notion that he fancies me and persuades me upstairs to dry off.

Childhood spaces are odd. Everything is strangely small but achingly familiar. Luggage commandeers one corner and the makeshift cot where I once slept has dishevelled bedclothes.

Raff darts about tidying. Breakfast dishes languish in the sink. The kitchen table contains sewing machine remnants.

"One of your efforts?" I say, surveying the debris.

He blushes and splutters. Our dynamics invert like a puddle reflection. Raff acting sheepish lends the impression that I, for once, possess greater confidence.

"It's a hobby," he croaks. "Dismantling and reassembling."

I clench as my mutinous body longs to disassemble beneath Raffaello.

He gestures for me to sit, provides a towel, then strips his soaked t-shirt and pulls on another. With Raff occupied rinsing an espresso pot, I excuse myself to use the bathroom.

My drenched appearance is a backhanded blessing. The least discerning fuck-and-chuck connoisseur wouldn't get it up for this bedraggled creature. And though I pine for someone's loving touch, I couldn't bear it if Raff used and discarded me, like so many of my lovers have before.

Returning with my hair in a towel turban, I find Raff waiting with coffees at the cluttered table. Here's hoping caffeine restores my equilibrium.

"What will happen when you get back to London?"

"I'll confront Nathan, I suppose, and ask about Daristan."

"You seek your real papa?"

"All my life I've chased acceptance by overachieving. Top grades at school to impress my dad. Master the cello. Join a jolly orchestra." My tongue flicks my lips. "Accomplishments don't erase loneliness."

Raff's brows pinch. "I crave home. You crave family." His chair legs scrape as he drags himself closer. "Your mamma's letter says you have your papa's hazel eyes. Even if you never find him, he lives in here."

His fingers press lightly over my heart.

"Quit being sweet to try and cop a feel," I scoff.

Withdrawing, he smiles softly. "Being nomadic is in your blood. Your Italian mamma leaves her homeland, marries a foreigner, and takes an immigrant lover. No surprise their daughter is fluent in music, a universal language."

Our pupils lock, magnetised. His gaze lowers to my mouth then bounces away as he jumps from his chair. While I steady myself, he puts a vinyl record on the turntable. The needle connects with a pop, crackle, hiss as the LP spins.

Otis Redding croons about lonely arms. I grin recalling my stocky Italian grandad practising English via soul records.

Raff's velvet vocals slice the atmosphere. "If music is language, dance is syntax."

The towel slips when I stand. Magnets fire again. Groins buff as hips shift into alignment. Hands circle my waist. Mine loop his neck. The graze of his chest electrifies my breasts.

Don't sully this friendship with sex, my mind cautions.

Stop overthinking, my loins retort. *Enjoy yourself for once. If Raff offers a one-off tumble, scratch your itch, have a meaningless fling. Others do it. Why can't you?*

"I never knew my papa," he murmurs. "But I know kinship when I feel it."

Need pulses in my veins. Music amplifies my thirst. Yearning and burning I hold Raff tight. His eyes resemble tempestuous skies. Omens of a storm ready to burst. Distance condenses as temptation grows. Jaws slant and mouths yield to gravity's pull.

His kiss is tender and potently intimate. His fingers splice my hair. I can't decipher who's in control. We move as one in hungry accord, exploring taste and touch as our tongues converge. When my jaw demands a break, passion-bruised lips convey my decision.

"Pull me apart, I'm yours to dismantle."

My offer is met with a husky growl. He kisses me harder than before. Hands slide to my backside. Mine echo their trajectory, clutching his bum. We haul our groins closer with a cheeky grope and grind. His erection nudges my abdomen. Rubbing against the male arousal I've stirred flushes liquid heat through my loins. Heartbreak be damned, I don't want to stop.

Usually, I'm anxious about getting naked. Yet here I stand in broad daylight feeling thoroughly shameless. I want Raff to appreciate the artistry and function of my female design. Time to increase gears. I break the seal on our kiss and in one fluid swoop, my top hits the floor.

The internal ache to receive Raff's thrust is almost too much. But other places crave his touch.

"Feel me," I say, arching my torso.

He abandons my rear to cup my crotch and cradle a breast. Lean fingers span my inseam and my silky bra. The jolt that assaults when he tweaks a stiff teat pitches my hips. Buried beneath denim and cotton, another needy flesh knot weeps for this treatment.

Contrasting everything lower than his chin, his expression is soft before he angles his head and kisses my neck. While lips tenderly nibble my skin, his hips piston a preview of coming attractions. My heart pounds, its pulse replicated between my legs.

Raff strokes me in places our younger selves never knew created such pleasurable sensations. Libidos revved and accelerating, he tugs my bra strap.

"This go?"

"If you're topless too."

He smirks and strips, unveiling sculpted pecs and abs. Swarthy body hair flecks his chest. Slithering to a narrow line at his navel, it plunges intriguingly. While busy painting a juicy mental picture, I whip off my bra.

Torrid snogging resumes to muffle our moans. But nothing restrains our roaming hands. Holy shit, gotta strap my mind in. Non-refundable tickets to the coitus-coaster means no getting off until we've loop-de-looped, conquered the summit and arrived fully sated at the docking station.

Bravado trounces trepidation. "Do you mind if I..." I pop his jeans' button and semi-lower his zipper.

He sucks on my tongue and rocks his hips. I hesitate until he brackets my wrist and positions my palm across his gloriously long and hard, thick dick. When Raff returns to massaging my breasts, I rub his shaft like a manic treasure hunter frantically seeking to uncork a genie.

"Careful!" he gulps, breaking our kiss.

Blimey, dial it down, desperado. No need to admit how long it's been.

"Sorry, I..."

"No, I love it, but I'm very excited. I don't want our first time to finish too quick."

First time implies a second. Possibly a third.

Settle petal. Keep it together.

The rejection when he chooses a blonde stick insect as my replacement will hurt like hell, but I won't die wondering how it felt to go all the way.

Now he's made our agenda clear, we move without words to the rumpled day bed. I unlace my sandals. He disposes of sneakers and socks. We ditch our jeans but leave our underwear on. Last gasp insurance policy in case we chicken out.

Raff fetches a foil square from his wallet and rips it open. His eyes search mine for affirmation that we're on the same page. Smiling, I take off my knickers and recline on the bed. He drags down his boxer briefs and kicks them away, then pincers the condom's tip and rolls it down his luscious length.

My head spins at the prospect of lying skin to skin with Raff Nardin. Although already horizontal, I might pass out.

He slots into the cradle of my thighs, fabricated for the ideal fit.

"Emelia," he exhales.

"I want this," I whisper.

Another untamed growl curls up his throat. Fingers caress my female sex. Sleek and ready, I writhe with needy sighs of encouragement. Aroused flesh enters mine, lighting me up as my body expands to welcome his cock.

Our noses buff and lips quiver as we build to a rhythm. Raff typically speaks with lucid conviction, as opposed to my mind which crafts constant chatter, then carefully edits what spills into the atmosphere. Bizarrely, in bed, we're the opposite.

Raff's vocab is trimmed to primal grunts. Incoherent cussing articulates his needs and responses. Whereas I verbalise the whole enchilada with the carnal candour of a phone sex worker.

Yes, Raff, drill there. Your speed is flawless, this angle divine. Fuck me, your dick's torque is magnificent! Now keep teasing my clit while moving inside me.

Who knew I possessed such a potty mouth? Or flexible joints.

My voice grows raspy. We're on the home straight. Perspiration dots Raff's brow. Like acrobatic tumblers we swap positions without slowing tempo. Now I'm on top and he's below. Scrambling to see who'll come first, I gyrate like a horny belly dancer, riding him hard to the finish line.

Gasps doused in shock and rolled in pleasure announce my climax. My spinal column stretches then arches. Raff's bucking stops with a final pelvic thrust. His hips still and he issues a pleasured groan, while I undulate through rolling waves of ecstasy. In case my orgasm milking his dick hasn't made it manifest, shuddering inside and out, I breathlessly chant, "I'm coming!" with every fresh spasm.

Raff's bedroom eyes latch to mine. Dreamy come-hither mists his gaze as my muscles relax around his twitches and pulses.

"*Porco dio!*" he gulps, sucking down air. "Em, seriously, you've broken my—"

"I broke it!" My dynamic dismount proves so spectacular I'm expecting an Olympic gymnast coach to call.

The appendage responsible for ravishing me adopts a lean to rival the Tower of Pisa. The latex sheathed rod is bloated with a creamy conditioner-like substance. Holy crap. Cum means that I made Raff come.

He chuckles. It bounces. I swear I go cross-eyed.

"You broke my mind. I've never had an orgasm so intense. And my heart..." His palm pats his chest at a quick trot while his smile erupts.

Dizzy with delight, I fear I'll cry or explode or possibly both.

"Be right back!"

I scurry to the bathroom to meltdown in private. Safe from prying eyes, I snatch a t-shirt off his laundry pile. It flaunts my curves but I've only eyes for the open journal lying on the counter flashing my name.

Ordinarily, catching your bonking partner washing their genitals at the kitchen sink might trigger misgivings. What I just read dwarfs dubious male hygiene as a red flag.

"What the hell is this?" I wave the journal, despising my obvious scratchy, distress.

He turns and squints. "*Scusa*. I took my contacts out."

"Forget about glasses, could you put on some pants, please!"

While he scrabbles to comply, I haul up my twisted knickers. Blowed if I'll have this conversation with my hoo-ha displayed. It takes serious unravelling to convert my underpants from a tourniquet. By the time I'm done, Raff stands in boxer briefs and translucent frames.

"My journal." His flustered tone and frown ratchets suspicion.

"Correct! Give the man a prize."

He pales at my outburst. Lucky for him I'm not holding scissors, though dick papercuts remain tempting.

"This was open on your London relocation notes."

"Em, I planned to tell you."

"Before or after you'd achieved dot point three: hook up with Emelia for fun times."

His eyebrows squirm like salted leeches.

"Aren't I easy prey!" Shit and bollocks, add stinging eyeballs to my squeaky voice. "Locked in your friends-with-benefits scheme, complete with London flat to crash, before moving onto a worthier girl."

"That's not my plan. When I say *fun*, you misunderstand—"

"Christ, Raffaello, you just literally screwed me! Don't screw me figuratively too. You know what *hook up* means."

I chuck the journal and grab my jeans. Serves me right for sleeping with someone named after his mum's favourite chocolate truffle.

"Emelia ..."

"I'm such a tool." *The apple doesn't fall far from the tree.*

"Working in London, I'm closer to mamma who's getting older. And when I heard about your nonno, I yearned for home and our summers together."

"Great, I'm a pity shag, profitable lay, and sentimental bonk rolled into one."

"Em, I swear, I didn't engineer this. I feel a strong connection with you—"

"Shut it, Raff! You had your *fun*, now let me go while I still have a shred of dignity."

I snatch my sandals, bra, and top, ramming them into my bag. The phrase *all I got was this lousy t-shirt* taunts as I march for the exit.

Raff blocks the way. "Please don't go."

"Says the boy who vanished from my life thirteen years ago!"

"That's not how I remember things. You chose music camps over summers here." He sprints and grabs his journal. "You want to know my private agenda? I write a journal every year. Give me an hour, I'll leave them downstairs. Read my thoughts before you judge me."

ᏣᏃᎠ

After walking off my strop, I return to Nonno's shop, wondering why someone this fit would go to such elaborate lengths to source a fuck buddy?

With Raff upstairs, I comb the journal entries he's marked for my attention. There wasn't enough time for doctoring. Hasty forgeries couldn't be this comprehensive.

As I skim his loopy scrawl — written in English to practise the language — I buff tears from my cheeks to prevent the ink blotting. Of my stupid misdeeds, wrongfully condemning a once-trusted friend ranks painfully high.

Found out Em isn't coming this year. Summer won't be the same missing her fun.

Sent a Christmas card to Emelia. Didn't get one back. Cello must keep her busy.

Goodbye Rome. Hello NYC. I wish Em could explore this city with me.

Time and again, his sweet reflections tug my heartstrings.

For seven summers, Emelia Russo was my best friend. Today I hear depressing news. Em's nonno died. I must fly home and pay my respects. Hopefully she remembers me fondly, like I do her.

My human heart's perplexing mechanics switch from chaotic to crystal clear. Overthrowing self-doubt, I scramble upstairs and pound Raff's door. He opens it, looking like the last puppy awaiting adoption.

I don't censor my thoughts. "For seven summers in a foreign city, I understood how it felt to belong, because of you."

His hands capture mine. He walks backwards and I follow, our fingers intertwined.

"Do you think home and family can reside inside a person of your choosing?"

He lifts my knuckles to his lips. "I think if we choose wisely, love makes anything possible."

Ancient Rome's innovations advanced civilisation. My advancement entails the life-changing innovation of following my heart without fear.

The next hour is a blur of pornographic proportion. Our second time transcends the first, as Raff's talented tongue takes me to multi-orgasmic nirvana.

Lying here panting, I've countless questions. For example, does he like post-sex snuggles? Should I call him my boyfriend? Further-bloody-more, how lucky am I?

He rolls over and delivers exquisite answers.

10

BURNING ASPHALT

KAREN LIEVERSZ

Lachie

I swear every vehicle in the Sydney metropolitan area is either bee-lining for a night out in the city or escaping to the country. Add a couple of accidents to screw up the carefully choreographed movement, and I'm trapped in the mother of all traffic jams with increasingly angry commuters. Horns blare. Brakes squeal. Screams of abuse fly through the air like scatter bombs. I want nothing more than to cuff all the crazy bastards and shove them into one giant cell until they calm the fuck down.

I shut the window, inhale a deep breath, and let the soothing strains of Mozart wash through me. This is why I prefer cruising the highways — just me and my patrol car, and the odd fool reckless enough to disobey the road rules on my watch.

The traffic lights turn green, and I crawl onto Oxford Street — and more of the same. Bloody hell. At this rate, it'll be midnight before I get home. Partygoers stroll along the footpath, seemingly oblivious to the traffic jam next to them.

A flash of red hair has my pulse quickening. I'd recognise those shoulder-length waves anywhere. It's my new next-door neighbour, Steve Haroldson. He's so close, I can make out the sky blue of his eyes.

My dick gives zero to a hundred a whole new meaning, and I adjust myself to release the pressure in my pants. I've imagined that exact shade of blue more times than I'd care to admit over the last two months as I've jacked off in the privacy of my bedroom. The bathroom. Hell, every room in the house, and there's nine of them if you count the laundry. Which I do.

Trouble is, Steve's given no sign he swings my way.

So, what's he doing here?

Steve catches me staring, and a cute flush creeps up his neck and across his cheeks. I smirk and wink. His hand flies to his throat, which bobs up and down like he's got something stuck in it. And just like that, my balls tighten.

A honking horn jolts my focus back to the road. I wave at Steve and press the accelerator, sneaking a glance in the rear-view mirror. His gaze is fixed on my vehicle, adding fuel to the flames licking my skin.

There's no way I'm going home now. I veer down a narrow side street and call up my best buddy.

"Hey, Charlie."

"Lachie." The tension in my muscles melts at the sound of Charlie's bubbly voice. "How are you, gorgeous?"

"Same as always. Working."

"Tut, tut. All work and no play makes Lachie a very dull boy." He chuckles. "And cranky."

"I'm not cranky."

"Not yet. But if you keep up the solo life much longer, no amount of physio will fix the damage to your right hand."

He's impossible. "Ha, ha. Real funny."

"Hey, I'm a doctor. I know these things." He lowers his voice. "But I get it. Sometimes, the best partner is your own company. So, what's up?"

"I thought I'd drop into the Stonewall Hotel. Any chance there's a spot outside your terrace I could park?"

"Yes!" Charlie squeals. "That's my boy."

"Just a drink, Charlie. Not a hook up."

"Honey, if you're wearing that police uniform of yours, you won't need to do any picking up. They'll come to you like bees—"

"Ouch." I shudder. "I don't want to be stung. And I changed at the station."

"Shame. I'd love to join you, but I'm about to start my shift at the hospital."

"That's okay. I only want your parking spot."

"You wound me."

I smile. No doubt the palm of Charlie's hand is covering his chest, his eyes flipped to the ceiling. He's such a drama queen.

"Yeah, yeah."

"I'm glad you're putting yourself back out there, Lachie. You've been pining after that neighbour of yours for too long."

"Thanks." My voice shakes. "Gotta go. See ya."

Charlie's too astute. If we keep talking, I'll end up confessing I'm taking my obsession with Steve to a whole new level.

Steve's toe to toe with a bouncer when I stroll up to the Stonewall. His biceps ripple as he jabs his finger towards the door. He's a mesmerising sight with those flashing blue eyes and fiery mane. It's a rare combination. One that has my fingers itching to smooth the creases in his brow.

"What's going on?" I ask in my deepest, *don't fuck with me*, police voice.

The bouncer ignores the implied command and grabs a fistful of my shirt.

I whip out my badge and shove it in his face.

He backs off, palms up in surrender. "Sorry, officer."

I quirk an eyebrow at Steve.

He bites his lip and lowers his gaze. "He won't let me and my friends in."

His voice rumbles through me like the engine of the B-double truck he drives. I grit my teeth. Now is not the time to sport another boner.

The bouncer widens his stance and crosses his brawny arms. "They're too drunk."

I scan Steve up and down, hovering at his denim-clad crotch for a split second longer than is polite, then lift my gaze to his. "Are you?"

"No." He squirms. "I've only had two beers."

"Not him." The bouncer shakes his head. "His friends. The ladies threw up in the gutter."

Two couples cling to each other, their eyes glassy.

I rest my hands on my hips. "Come on, Steve. The bouncer's right."

"Fine." The woman closest to me flicks long blonde hair from her face. "We're never gonna get Steve laid here, anyway."

Steve's cheeks turn bright red.

I tilt my head. With sleek muscles and a ginger scruff I'd give anything to rub against, he couldn't possibly need help finding someone to warm his bed.

"You looking for a one-night stand?"

"No, no." He shakes his head so fast I almost get dizzy.

"He needs to," says the woman. "Spends too many hours in that truck of his. No girlfriend."

I clench my fingers. "So, you brought him to a gay bar?" Some friends.

She shrugs her shoulders. "There are other straight people here, too."

I roll my eyes. Seems Steve's companions are more interested in their own titillation than in helping him get lucky. "How about you guys get a taxi? I'll take Steve home."

Steve steps back, waving his hands. "No, no. You don't have to do that."

"It's no trouble. You live next door."

The blonde woman steps closer. "Ooh... is this the cop you were telling us about?"

Interesting. My smile broadens. "What have you been saying, Steve?"

"Nothing."

The flush in Steve's cheeks extends down his neck. It's adorable, and I can't help wondering how far it spreads.

"He said you were good looking, but he never mentioned how smoking hot you are." The woman stretches red-tipped fingers toward me. "You can use your handcuffs on me anytime, big boy."

I bite my tongue and side-step her grabby hands. She's touched a nerve. Too many people don't see me, just the uniform, even when I'm not wearing it. I didn't mind so much when I was younger. It got me laid. A lot. But I want more than casual sex now. It's one of the reasons I'm on a dating hiatus. Steve's the other one.

Her partner's eyes widen, and he yanks her away. "No problem. We'll catch a cab." He winks at Steve and gives me a lopsided grin. "Take good care of our mate."

My stomach flips. By 'good care', I doubt Steve's friend means the X-rated video playing in my mind right now.

Steve and I cross the road, our arms accidentally brushing against each other. That's all it takes for my dick to start throbbing in my pants. Or it could be the heady scent of his cologne that has me jacked up.

Steve tugs at the top of his shirt and stops. "Are you gay?"

Jesus. He's more forward than I expected. I halt mid-stride.

"Yes."

Steve gapes at me.

I smile. "Your mouth's hanging open."

He snaps it shut. "Sorry. I didn't think you'd admit it."

"I'm not ashamed." A tickle scratches at my throat. "But that doesn't mean I go around telling everyone my private business."

"Of course." Steve's blue eyes darken, and his gaze drops to my crotch.

I itch to ask him if he's gay too, but he drops his head and continues down the footpath.

Steve's quiet on the drive home, responding with monosyllables to my attempts at conversation. Heat prickles across my skin. I feel his gaze on me, but every time I peek at him, he's staring straight ahead. Maybe he's never been alone with a guy he knows likes men? Or maybe he's interested? I give myself a mental slap. That's wishful thinking gone crazy.

I pull into my driveway and kill the engine. Steve's throat does the bobbing thing that gets my dick twitching. He fumbles with the seat belt and turns to face me, his eyes bright. "Thanks for the ride, Lachlan."

"Please, it's Lachie." I place my palm on his shoulder. "Only my mum calls me Lachlan."

Steve nibbles at his bottom lip, his gaze dropping to my mouth. Heat radiates through the thin fabric of his shirt and into my hand.

My dick flies to full mast. *Fuck. Could he be into me?*

"It was no problem." I slide my palm down the furry skin of his arm until I reach his bicep and curl my fingers gently around the taut muscle. "I was happy to help."

Steve's pupils widen to shimmering black holes encased by blue so pure it's blinding. Instead of pushing me away, he places his hand on my thigh and squeezes. My dick punches painfully against the zipper of my trousers. There's no mistaking his intention.

A whiff of his spicy aftershave sends a fresh wave of blood to my aching groin. I lean closer and swipe my tongue across his lips. He whimpers. I swallow his gasps and press my lips against his. They're soft and warm, and I know with every fibre of my being, he's everything I've been looking for. His tongue flicks out to meet mine. Tentative at first. I groan, tangling my tongue with his, the faint taste of hops and mint making me hungry for more. Much more. I clasp the hand that's on my leg and slide it upwards. Steve's calloused fingers curl around the bulge in my trousers. My dick jerks in anticipation.

And then it all goes to shit.

Face flushed, Steve scrambles away, panting like he's run a marathon. "What the hell was that?"

My throat constricts. I didn't force myself on him, did I? "Sorry. I thought..."

My lungs strain as I gulp for air. Fuck. Fuck. Fuck. How did I read this so wrong?

Steve grabs the door handle and presses the palm of his right hand against his heaving chest.

"Nah, not your fault." He shakes his head. "I don't know what came over me. This isn't..." He waves at my crotch. "Me."

I nod. It seems safest to avoid any words at this point.

His lips twist. "Can we forget this ever happened?"

I nod again. "Sure." *No fucking way.* He's my every wet dream come to life.

He slides out of the car and sprints across the front lawn.

I slump back in my seat. What the hell just happened?

გვფა

Steve

I pace the living room while butterflies play a game of skirmish in my stomach. I can't believe Lachie's giving me a second chance. Not after the way I ran out on him last week.

Roast chicken sizzles in the oven. Not a supermarket cooked one, but a bird I stuffed myself, together with roast potatoes, carrots and onions. It's not real fancy, but it's the only meal I can cook without it turning into a triple zero call. It used to impress the women I dated. I'm hoping it'll have a similar impact on Lachie.

I've placed a candle and flowers from the garden in the centre of the table. Is that normal for two blokes, or is it only something you do with a woman? I wring my hands out, sweat trickling down my back. Damn. I should have googled it.

A sharp tap on the door has my heart slamming against my rib cage. Too late now.

My hands tremble as I greet Lachie. He stands tall, golden curls cropped short, his freshly shaved face making him look young and innocent. But there's nothing virtuous about the gleam in his hazel eyes. It's all man. I swallow, words lost somewhere at the bottom of my throat, and usher him in.

Lachie strides into the combined lounge/dining room, wisps of sandalwood and pine drifting in his wake. My legs wobble at the provocative scent.

His fingers skim across the ivory damask tablecloth. "You've gone to a lot of trouble."

I shake my head. "It's the least I could do after the way I acted."

"Not your fault." Lachie steps away from the table and clears his throat. "I came on too strong."

I let out a deep breath, one I didn't even know I was holding. We're just two guys. Eating a meal together. I can do this.

Dinner passes in a blur. We discuss the rush we both get driving on the freeways. I wasn't sure I'd have anything in common with a cop, but there's no denying our love of powerful engines.

After clearing the plates, I select a tune on Spotify. Tension eases from my shoulders at the soft, lilting piano.

Lachie stands in the kitchen doorway, his brows furrowed. "I wouldn't have picked you for a classical man."

Crap. Will I ever learn? My last girlfriend told me often enough how shitty my taste in music was, among other things.

I snatch my phone off the coffee table. "Would you rather I put some heavy rock on?"

"No. Definitely not." Lachie's fingers snake around my wrist. "Moonlight Sonata is perfect."

"You're not just saying that?"

"Nope. I'm more of a Mozart man, but Beethoven's good too."

Lachie's thumb rubs against my pulse.

Electricity zips up my arm and down my thigh. "That's surprising."

"Steve, it's okay to be yourself with me. I love classical music. It's all I listen to when I'm driving my patrol car."

"Me too." I pull away from the magic of his caress. "When I'm in my truck, of course, not a police car."

Great. Now I'm babbling. Way to impress.

Lachie smiles. "Do you want to sit down?"

I nod, and we sink onto the lounge. Lachie drapes his arm across its back and rests his hand on my shoulder.

My cock stiffens, and I freeze.

"We can take this as slow as you need, Steve." Lachie rubs the nape of my neck, seeming to sense my uncertainty. "Nothing has to happen tonight if you don't want it to."

Shit. I need to get over myself. I rub my palms down my thighs. "I have this fantasy."

Lachie leans closer, his eyes glittering. "Yeah?"

I gulp. How the hell do I tell him? "It's just... this is all new to me." I wave my hand at his groin and then mine. "I... I think I'd like to be forced."

Lachie's eyebrows climb up his forehead, and he withdraws his arm. "*Forced?*" His voice cracks. "What do you mean?"

Blood rushes to my head. Goddammit. This is so embarrassing. "It's hard to admit I like men. That I like you."

He nods, encouraging me, although shields seem to slide down his eyes.

"I find your police uniform a real turn on." I dig my fingers into my legs. Am I really going to say this? "Um... If you pretended to be a cop, which obviously you are, and um... told me I had to do things. Then..." Ah, crap. My face burns. "Forget it." I jump to my feet.

"No!" Lachie leaps off the sofa too. "Keep going."

"I'm thinking, if my first time was with you throwing orders at me, I might be able to, you know." I shrug my shoulders. "Loosen up."

"Let me get this straight." Lachie's face is impenetrable. Like granite. "You want me to order you to have sex with me? Like you're being punished for committing a crime?"

I shuffle my feet. I'm sure my cheeks must be bright red. "Yeah."

His eyes narrow.

Not the reaction I'd hoped for.

"This is not how it works, Steve." Storm clouds flit across Lachie's irises. "If you need games to get you going, then you're not ready."

"But I am. You're hot as fuck in your uniform."

"Yeah. I think maybe that's all you see. Trouble is..." Lachie's voice drops to a whisper. "I want more."

He grazes my cheek with his finger, pivots and walks out.

I crash on the lounge and hang my head in my hands. What a mess.

CR8D

"Fuuuck!"

The guttural cry reverberates across the airwaves and fills the cabin of my truck. I grip the steering wheel tighter, eyes fixed on the road. I can't afford to lose concentration at this speed, especially not in the dark.

"Fuck, yeah!"

Someone has left their radio on while jerking off, and the whole CB world will be eager to find out who it is so they can make their life hell. There's a rush of noise that suggests the person is driving. Who'd be crazy enough to do that? If I had any sense of decency, I'd turn off the radio and pretend I hadn't heard those cries of pleasure. But I don't. And neither will anyone else.

I pull my rig across from the middle of the freeway to the left lane and slow down to sixty kilometres an hour. So what if I'm late home? My cock is rigid as steel. It's been that way since I stuffed up my dinner date with Lachie three nights ago. I don't know how to make things right with him.

I yank the zipper down and pull myself free. Thank God I went commando this morning. I stroke the swollen length, smearing pre cum along the sides.

"Uh... uh..."

Fuck. I pull harder as that gravelly voice cries out. An image of Lachie in his cop car flashes in my mind. The zipper of that blue uniform undone, his cock sticking out. He'd have one foot on the accelerator, like me. One hand on the wheel. He'd be slumped in his seat, eyes half-lidded, watching the road while he stroked. Up and down. Down and up. Squeezing.

My balls tighten. I'm close to spilling my load.

"Oh, God. Yes."

Ah, crap. The bloke on the CB is coming. I can't hold back. I spurt cum everywhere. Onto the windscreen, the steering wheel, my jeans.

The truck shudders to a halt.

The next thing I know, blue lights flash in the rear vision mirror. Shit. I zip my pants, grab some tissues, and wipe up the mess.

The police car door opens. It's Lachie.

He swaggers to the cab of my truck, his lips pressed into a thin line.

I wind down the window and play it cool. "Hey, Lachlan."

"Step out of the vehicle, please sir."

Uh oh. He's using police speak on me. Surely I'm not in trouble. I wasn't speeding. Then again, I am stopped in the left-hand lane with no hazard lights on.

"Please alight from the vehicle. I won't ask you again."

His husky voice zips straight to my cock, and the traitorous appendage stirs in my jeans. I open the door and climb down from my truck.

My feet barely touch the ground before Lachie grabs me in a chokehold and flattens me against the side of the truck. What the hell? He kicks my legs apart. I dare not move.

"So, Mr Haroldson, why have you stopped?" He glances up into the cabin.

Shit. Can he see my jiz everywhere?

His gaze narrows to my crotch. I wriggle.

"Your pants are stained, Mr Haroldson. What caused that stain?"

His eyes are dark, glittering gemstones stripping me naked as his gaze travels up to my burning face.

"Ah, nothing. Just coffee." My pulse skyrockets. He's so hot when he's all cop-like. This is what I meant the other night. Before he stormed out of my house. Dom/sub stuff has always intrigued me.

He peers into the cabin of the truck again. "I don't see any cups. Don't lie to me, Mr Haroldson. You wouldn't lie to a police officer now, would you?"

"No, no." I swallow. "Of course not."

Lachie looks around. "This isn't a safe place to stop. Get back in your truck and drive to the next exit. There's a clearing you can pull into when you get there."

"Yes, sir."

My legs are like jelly as I climb into the truck.

Is this police business or something else?

I drive to the spot Lachie mentioned, super aware of the police car behind me. My parking lights cast an eerie red glow that mingles with the dark shadows of the deserted rest area. I climb out of the truck and hand Lachie my wallet.

He shakes his head. "I won't need that."

"What do you want, then?"

"For you to drop your pants."

My jaw collapses, and if my eyes weren't connected to their sockets, they'd be eating dirt.

"I have reason to believe you were masturbating while driving. I need to inspect your dick."

"What the hell?"

Lachie's hands fly to his hips. "Are you defying a direct order?"

I'm sure my mouth must be flapping in the breeze like one of those clowns at the show. Is he playing out my fantasy? Am I reading this right?

"Oh God... what a shame."

Lachie says the words all breathy. My body goes rock hard and my cock even harder, if that's possible.

"It was you on the CB?"

"Yeah." He smirks. "Me."

"Why?"

"You're all I think about." He sighs and rakes a hand through his hair. "And your fantasy reminded me of mine."

"To jerk off on the radio?"

He nods.

My stomach flips, and electricity dances across my skin. "Or did you just pretend?"

"Oh no. It was for real." He shakes his head and grins. "If you drop your pants and show me the cum all over your dick, I'll show you mine."

Jesus. My cock weeps at the husky promise in his voice.

Lachie's smile widens as his gaze drops to my crotch. "Are you going to pull those jeans down or not?"

I rip the button open and yank at the zipper. My cock springs free, a white pearl dripping at the tip.

Lachie licks his lips. "I over-reacted the other night. There's nothing wrong with playing games, especially with the right partner."

He gives me a look that burns deep into my soul and promises to keep me safe. "But the choice is yours. You don't have to go through with it if you don't want to."

I clear my throat. This is it. No more excuses. It's time to embrace what I want or stay miserable.

"No, no. I'm good. Have your way with me, officer. I've been bad. Very bad, and I deserve to be punished."

Especially if punished means a blow job or a good fucking. My stomach clenches. At least I think I'm ready for a good fucking. Crap. I'm not sure.

Lachie gestures to the cab of the truck. "After you."

"You don't want me bent over?"

"Fuck, yeah." His eyes darken. "But your first time doing anal shouldn't be on the side of the road."

Lachie herds me toward the open door, and I clamber onto the bed behind the driver's seat. Not an easy feat with my pants dangling around my knees. He looms over me, one hand on my chest, the other stroking my jaw. His face is so close; his exhale becomes my inhale. Sandalwood and pine tickle my nose. He licks along the crease of my lips, and I part them, granting him entry. My cock throbs with every stroke of his tongue inside my mouth. If he keeps it up, I'll come before he gets anywhere near my crotch.

His lips leave mine and nuzzle a path down my jaw and neck to the sensitive hollow at my collarbone. He bites down, and I jerk against him.

"Fuck! Lachie."

He soothes the sting with soft, wet kisses. "Shh. It's okay." He lifts his head. "Are you ready?"

"Yeah," I murmur. "More than ready." I feel like I've been waiting all my life for this moment. For Lachie.

He pulls a condom from his pocket. I seize his hand. "I don't want anything between us."

Lachie's eyebrow lifts. I don't blame him for looking sceptical. Protection is non-negotiable.

"I got tested after my last girlfriend," I say quickly. "It was negative."

"I see." Lachie's lips curl into a wickedly delicious grin. "I'm good to go, too. I did a test shortly after you moved in next door. There's been no one since."

Really?

Lachie crawls down my body and cups my balls, squeezing all rational thought from my brain. He lowers his head and nibbles my cock from tip to root and back again. His tongue swirls wickedly around the head, licking up the remnants of my earlier solo effort.

"Fuck, you taste good, Steve."

I groan at the raspy sound of Lachie's voice, his blond head bobbing between my legs.

He takes me further into his blistering wet mouth and sucks harder than I've ever been sucked. Stars dot across my vision. Holy shit. I buck against him and come with a roar, pumping down his throat.

My breath is ragged, my body pulsing. I haven't come so quickly since I was a randy teen. Lachie takes his time licking and sucking, cleaning up every drop of cum. His touch is soft and reverent. He stretches over me until we're chest to chest. Cock to cock. Lips to lips. He tastes of me and of the spicy sandalwood that is him. It's as intimate as what we've just done. Maybe more so.

"Was it okay?" he whispers in my ear.

"Better than okay."

"Excellent." He smiles. "I'm on duty, so I need to go. Can I see you tomorrow night?"

"Absolutely." I'm dying to reciprocate.

"Just one thing." The hard glitter returns to his eyes.

My pulse quickens. "Yeah?"

"I don't think you've been punished enough for your misdemeanour. I'll bring handcuffs."

My spent cock twitches. Jesus. Never in my wildest dreams did I imagine it could be this good. And it's all thanks to this man.

He gives me another chaste kiss then climbs out of the truck.

I pull up my jeans and settle into the driver's seat. The radio dangles on the floor. Has it been on? I'm sure I turned it off.

"Testing..."

"Hellooo, lover."

"Ah, crap."

"Don't be shy. We appreciated the show. Between what sounded like the blow job of the century and the other bloke rubbing one out, there isn't a dry trucker on the roads tonight."

Howls of laughter erupt from the radio. Another five minutes of ribald jokes, and I've had enough. I flick it off and manoeuvre onto the freeway. The rumble of the engine and Vivaldi's Four Seasons fill the cabin.

This is the life. Just me and my truck. The musky scent of sex and Lachie. And the promise of more. So much more.

Lachie

I cruise along the empty freeway, the lingering taste of Steve on my tongue, my dick semi-hard. BDSM hasn't done it for me before, but with Steve, it feels right. If he likes the handcuffs tomorrow night, I wonder if he'll enjoy a paddle? Or a ball gag?

My dick swells. I don't want to get ahead of myself, but I've got a good feeling.

I call up Charlie.

"Lachie, how are you, sweetness?" he croons down the line.

"Good. Real good."

"Ooh. I like the sound of that. You get yourself some action that didn't involve your right hand?"

"Yes." I chuckle. "I did."

"So, you're back in the saddle?"

"Sort of."

"What do you mean?"

"I gave Steve a blow job, but I've still got a huge case of blue balls."

The whoosh of tyres on asphalt fills my ears.

"Charlie? Are you there?"

"Sorry, sweetie." He sniffles. "I'm just a bit emotional. My little boy's growing up."

I squint at the road ahead of me as if that will help me understand. "What the fuck are you talking about?"

"I've been worried about your obsession with Steve, but you gave without taking. That's a sign, my friend."

"Yeah, a sign I don't want to scare him off. Besides, I enjoyed tasting him." Remembering his little grunts, dick swelling in my mouth, his total submission. I adjust my pants. "It was hardly one-sided."

"You dress it up however you need to."

Fucking Charlie. I clench the steering wheel. There's no fooling him. He knows me too well.

A Subaru WRX screams past like I'm standing still. I hit the accelerator. The engine doesn't miss a beat as the car surges forward.

"Sorry, Charlie. Got to go. Love ya."

"Love you too, sweetie. Don't be shy. I want to meet the man who's captured your heart."

I flip on the siren, drowning out the peaceful strains of Mozart. The arsehole in the Subaru is in for a rude shock. No one breaks the rules on my watch and gets away with it. Except for Steve. My pants tighten. But he'll willingly pay for it later. Cuffed to my bed.

II

THRUSTING OPEN AN INVISIBLE DOOR

BRIDGET W DEEN

"**A**re you ready?"

"Of course! I styled my hair and everything."

"Are you taking this seriously? This is extremely dangerous!"

"Excuse me. My hair is a serious matter. I want you to witness me in my prime."

"You're impossible."

"And you're adorable when you're worried. See you on the other side, my love."

∞

"How long do I have?" I asked, fingering the cold metal cuff that had been slapped onto my wrist.

The woman responsible for placing it there sat crossed legged on the wooden floor, hunched over a large metal suitcase laid flat and open to reveal a supercomputer of her own design. Danii, a physics and inter-dimensional engineering genius, looked up and shrugged.

"Don't know. An hour, maybe six. Could be a week."

Great. I loved her confidence.

She glanced back at the computer. It was buzzing and flashing like a party was being held inside of it. "It depends on the distance between our dimension and the dimension I'm connecting you and your stalker to."

"He's not a — never mind," I said, once again fiddling with the metal that was scratching against my sensitive pale skin. Danii shook her head, her hijab holding steady as she continued to work her magic on the keyboard under her fingers, while I paced the floor of the living room. All the pent-up energy inside of me needed somewhere to go and moving back and forth between the fraying couches and the tea-stained coffee table was helping to dissipate it.

My stomach was a tangle of knotted thread, my chest so tight it stung. Danii was going to put her lucrative work to the test, and I was going to come face to face with the invisible figure that had been haunting my home since the day my world had crumbled to ash, literally. Though haunting was a loose term to describe my phantom's actions.

Very loose.

As Danii fiddled away, I replayed the memories of all the actions that had led me to be here. Ever since I was a little kid I'd felt unwanted. A burden passed around between foster families, unable to feel a moment of secure happiness unless surrounded by animals of every kind. But I'd never fully hit rock bottom until last year.

A year ago, my abusive ex-boyfriend Gale burned my life to the ground. A year ago, my beautiful veterinary business was set aflame, destroying *everything* inside of it. Destroying *me*.

And a year ago... another man came to my rescue.

Too depressed to even move, Quillon found me at my lowest. He was an invisible figure with a solid touch and intense desire to see me smile. Gale had never known about the house in the woods that my birth mother had given to me upon her death. I hadn't either, not until fate had handed me the key and opened the door, revealing an unusual feature that the real-estate agent had forgot to mention.

There was a tear in it.

Not on the wallpaper, or in the floorboards, but in the air. An opening between dimensions.

"Aluma, stop moving." I stopped at Danii's request and pulled my fingernails from my mouth. I'd started chewing without even noticing. Hopefully they weren't bleeding just yet. Quillon disliked it when I did that. My body heated at the thought of his name.

Danii played with a few buttons on a large touch screen then stood, her boots shuffling across the floor so she could place another cuff in my hands. "This one is for your... friend," she said. I appreciated that she hadn't referred to him as a stalker again. "I just hope you're right and he's definitely not a ghost." Her youthful green eyes found mine, a hint of worry evident in the way she chewed her lower lip. We were both as nervous as each other.

I helped her move the coffee table into the hallway and proceeded to put all of my homemade vases away in case they shattered. "He's not a ghost," I reminded her confidently. "I've told you this already. The first night he spoke to me, I went and bought a shit tonne of sage and burnt it all night. In the morning he had written *I'm not a ghost* on my mirror."

"How?"

"With lipstick."

"What kind of psycho wastes lipstick like that?" she said, and I smiled, my eyes zeroing in on her bold pink lips.

Once the living room was free of obstacles, Danii went to sit by her computer again and I stood in the centre of the worn floorboards trying to calm myself. Seconds later I felt a warm rush of air slide down my neck. It smelled of storm clouds and cedar. Of strength and an essence of power that was foreign to our world but had become so familiar to me.

He was here. Waiting.

Thunder boomed beyond the mountains as Danii finalised her equations. Through the closed curtains I could make out the distant snap of lightning, the pounding of incoming rain. The perfect conditions to connect dimensions and make my ghost a reality.

My hands began to tremble as the balmy presence of him pushed up against my back. The phantom fingers I had come to know so intimately stroked my stomach, and glided down the outside of my arms. A rush of goosebumps followed wherever he touched. I swallowed a moan when the light pressure of his fingertips pressed between my legs at the same time his lips found the sensitive skin of my neck.

In my right ear he whispered, "Not long now."

"Alright. I'll be ready to go in ten minutes. Once the storm is above us I'll activate the Fold and pray it works," Danii said, wiping her hands vigorously on her jeans.

I nodded, a bubble of dread expanding in my stomach. Danii had warned me of the dangers and still I'd pestered her; begged her to try and do it. I knew it was selfish, reckless. But after a year of being comforted by an invisible entity, I was determined to finally discover the man who had made me laugh when I wanted the world to swallow me whole.

The walls of the house shook as the thunder intensified and, as time ticked on, I distracted myself by running to the bathroom and checking my appearance. I made sure that my strawberry blonde hair was still wavy, that my mascara wasn't flaking, that the jeans and white shirt that hugged my curvy frame hadn't suddenly been stained with my sweat. It was a pointless endeavour. Quillon could already see me. But either way, I looked fine. Albeit a little jumpy.

Shivering with anticipation, I ran my fingers over my mirror. Over the script of elegant handwriting crawled along the surface in the only red lipstick I owned.

I can't wait to hold you properly.

My heart raced at the idea of seeing the hands that wrote these words. At hearing them fall from his lips. At seeing him whole and real and ready.

I checked my cuff to see whether a timer had begun. Three minutes left and counting. I marched out of the bathroom and towards Danii who was waiting besides the groaning machine.

"Can I ask you a question?" I said. Danii kept her focus on the computer but nodded for me to continue. "Is it possible for me to go back with him?"

Her perfectly trimmed brows furrowed for a second as she thought. "Yes. It's possible. You will have to be touching each other, and both have to press the button on your cuffs at the same time to be released from this world."

The stiffness in my chest eased slightly. There was a chance he could take me away. I knew it was a silly thought — a thought that made me feel a little weak — but if there was nothing left for me here, why should I stay?

Danii checked the timer and dropped to a kneeling position. "Alright. It's time. Stand in the centre of the room and get the cuff ready to put on his wrist. And if you start to feel like your skin is burning, get away from the entrance zone."

I nodded, bending my legs, and straightening my spine. I chanced a quick look at the timer on my cuff. Thirty seconds.

Lightning sparkled behind the fabric curtains, bathing the space in quick slashes of white. My ears roared with the thumping of rain on the metal roof. Danii began to count down.

Ten.

My heart stuttered. The machine roared to life. Fingers grazed against my cheek.

Nine.

Sweat dripped under my arms; my knuckles went white from holding the cuff too tight.

Eight. Seven.

The screen on the machine beeped and buzzed. A tiny light began to form in the air in front of me.

Six.

I stopped breathing.

Five.

The tiny dot, almost like a star, began to burn and build in size. Glowing brighter than any light I had ever seen.

Four. Three.

Danii grunted and I saw in the corner of my eyes her fingers flying over the screen, her lips thin, her eyes worried.

Two.

I stepped back. The orb was bigger now, the size of my head. It was so bright I had to squint to see clearly.

One.

Everything seemed to pause, to hold. And then... *Bang!*

Lightning struck the roof. I gasped and fell to my knees. An explosion ripped through the room. My entire body shook. I couldn't see anything. The ball of dazzling light had blinded me. Danii shouted my name.

Everything went black.

The machine died. The power went out. Even the few candles I had burning in the kitchen sputtered and smoked.

"Shit," Danii said, but my ears were still ringing slightly.

I looked up to see nothing but darkness. My heart plummeted to the bottom of my stomach. I fisted my hands into my belly to keep myself from crumbling apart. I wanted to scream. I wanted to punch my hand through a wall.

I wanted to see Quillon just *once*.

As my knees went weak and my heart shattered to pieces, I felt the energy in the room begin to shift. My skin prickled with heat and the hair on my head seemed to turn heavy.

Lightning struck the roof again with a savage crack, but this time I was ready. The entire room burst into a kaleidoscope of colour. Shapes danced about; light snapped and twisted.

I took a step forward. The light was now circling and spinning and forming into something physical. I raised my arm to shield my face as I continued to move forward, my heart pounding frantically, on the verge of popping from excitement.

The storm grew frenzied outside, but I couldn't hear anything once my eyes looked onto the body forming before me. A man. He was shadow and sun. Liquid and solid. He was lifting his arm out to me. I pushed on, ignoring the fact that my skin was sizzling, the hairs on my arm burning. I kept going, determination and desire forcing me to see this through. I held the cuff open until it was hovering above the outline of a wrist. I couldn't make out the details, but I knew it was his.

Danii screamed something. The machine sounded like it was going to erupt.

I ground my teeth, pushed through the pain and snapped the cuff onto the arm. I pressed the button right before I felt my vision go black around the edges.

A force sent me flying backwards. I landed in a heap on the couch, the breath knocked from my lungs.

I opened my eyes to see the light in the room had focused completely on one person.

Quillon.

I gasped, unable to move. I was too struck by the size of him. By the width of his chest, the length of his legs, the cutting angles of his face contrasted against his soft, pink mouth.

Just *him*. Real and alive and standing before me like some awesome god from another world.

I heard a groan and spun to see Danii leaning against the wall connecting to the kitchen. Her hijab had slipped back.

I found my legs and launched across the room to check if she was okay. She managed a small smile as I reached for her. "Are you alright?" I asked and she waved me off.

"Yes, yes I—" Her gaze travelled to what was behind me. "You — your. Aluma. He's— he's—"

"Hello Danii," he said, and my entire body turned to liquid.

Holy shit. His voice was nothing like it had been when he was held back by forces of the universe. Now it was startlingly clear, as rich and as smooth as the finest whiskey, and powerful enough to force my thighs together.

I stood slowly, turning to see him watching me. Bright, grey eyes connected with mine. He was even bigger than I'd hoped. Towering over me with what could only be described as thick, corded muscle underneath his casual ensemble. A deep navy shirt covered his upper body, the two buttons at the top undone, his pants looked like jeans but somehow I knew they weren't. His deep brown hair was swept back into a ponytail, wisps of it surrounded his cheeks, his shoulders. His eyes appeared to be lined with something black and one of his ears was covered in jewellery.

Had I been living with a pirate from another dimension this entire time? I wanted to shriek in delight. Why did it matter? He could have been a monster and I still would have crumbled at his feet.

Quillon was sexy as fuck. And I shouldn't have been surprised, because he'd told me as much, on multiple occasions.

Danii stood behind me and reached for my fingers. "He's real," she said. "I did it!" I squeezed her hand. "I'll give you two some space. I just need to fix something with the Fold." Danii made some quick adjustments to the machine still in operation while Quillon and I continued to observe each other. Drink each other in.

Finally, she stood. "You have about twelve hours before the dimensions split you apart. I've started a countdown on your cuffs." I felt the urge to smash my cuff against a wall. Danii hesitated and then whispered to me. "The machine should stay stable. I'll be at the hotel. Call me if something happens."

She quickly grabbed her bag and headed for the door, but not before turning around and looking Quillon straight in the eyes. "If you hurt her, you bet your ass I'll be hunting you down for the rest of my life. I know where you came from, bitch."

A cough escaped my lips as I moved towards her to give her a hug, even though I knew it wasn't her thing. I would be forever grateful for her brain and her generosity. "If I'm gone when you come back. Tell everyone I died happy."

"I will," she said and smiled meekly. "Be safe, Aluma." And then she was gone. Running through the storm that suddenly didn't seem so big. I closed the door, a tiny ache in my heart at the notion that I might never see her again.

I wandered back to the living room to where Quillon stood, my steps faltering as I neared him. This was beyond strange. Crazy. And yet nothing had ever felt so natural. At what point was it okay for me to throw myself into his chest?

"I'm not scared of much, but she scares me," he said, and the comment was enough to snap the tension out of the room.

I ran a shaky hand through the waves of my hair, no doubt now limp and messy. "I can't believe she did it."

Quillon remained quiet for a few beats and then his voice rumbled across the distance between us. "Hello to you too," he said, and my pulse tripled its frantic cadence.

"Hi."

He smiled, just a bit, and the tightening in my chest detonated into a million sparkling particles. "Aluma, come here."

My feet moved of their own accord. He was the sand, and I was the ocean, forever magnetised to be near his presence. Only before it had been imaginary, now he was hot and solid before me.

He didn't reach for me, simply watched as I closed the distance between us. The heat of his skin burned into mine and I felt my body sway and tremble just from being so close to him.

His grey eyes skimmed over every inch of my face, as if he couldn't believe I was real. But this moment *was* real, and I was desperate to connect beyond our minds as we had been for the last year. I wanted to feel him up against me, behind me, inside me.

Everywhere.

"You are such a gift," he said, barely a whisper. He ran his fingers down the side of my face. I ran my tongue over my lips. "Are you not going to put on a show for me tonight, now that we are finally together?" he asked, playing with the ends of my hair. My core was pulsing. Thumping. I wanted his big hands on my skin, gripping and tight.

"That was *one* time," I said, shivering at the memory of playing with myself as he had watched from wherever he had been hidden, his voice rough and hungry in my ear, urging me to an explosive climax that left my knees shaking for hours.

"But I want an encore."

I laughed and lifted my fingers to touch the rings and jewels embedded in his ear. None of my musings, my dreams, had done him justice.

"And I want…"

"Yes? What do you want?"

My future suddenly didn't seem so dark with him standing

beside me. So, I decided I was going to be brutally honest. I looked him straight in the eyes and said, "I want you to strip me naked and fuck me for the next twelve hours or however long I have you. I want you to hold me and hug me and kiss me. I want you every way I possibly can. Every way that I've been starved of this last year."

His smile turned positively wicked. "Done, done and done." I gulped, wishing liquid into my suddenly dry mouth and a way to bottle his musky scent for me to use as a perfume. "I'll make every second worth your while, Aluma. I'll make you *come* in every possible way I know and then I'll hold you against me until the final second falls."

I was hot and cold and utterly *desperate*. "What are you waiting for?"

"For you to kiss me Aluma. Where I come from—" I didn't give him a chance to finish. I rose to my toes and leaped the distance between us. I brought my lips to his and wrapped my hands around his thick neck. Our bodies clashed together, and I moaned at the hardness of him, the fucking incredible feeling of his groin pressed against mine, of his hands at my back forcing us closer.

It was not a gentle claiming. Quillon devoured me with his mouth. His lips and tongue and hands moved with a ferocity that I craved in every part of my skin, my bones, my heart.

I had wished for this moment since the first time we conversed, when he had placed a blanket around my shoulders and asked me to tell him what had made me so sad.

"I've lost everything."

"But not yourself, you are right here."

"It doesn't feel like it."

"I see you. And I know it hurts, but it won't last forever. Tell me what makes you laugh."

His rumble of approval as I snaked my hands into his hair was enough to have me shoving him backward and into a wall. He laughed into my mouth. "You're so strong. It's my favourite thing about you, and it means I'll be able to fuck you hard enough and not be scared of breaking you."

My response was a deep, hearty moan. I pulled at his shirt, the metal cuff on my wrist digging and scraping. When the buttons wouldn't budge, he let go of me to rip his shirt clean off. Mine was gone a second later, followed by my lacy bra in one quick swipe of his fingers.

He brought our bare chests together and we moaned in unison. He began to kiss me again, one hand wrapped around my back, the other tracing my nipples, cupping my breasts, squeezing. Before I knew it, his hand was snaking down my stomach and under my jeans. When his fingers flicked the lining of my underwear, I jerked and lost all control of my body. "I know you're not human, but you must be some type of sex god."

He chuckled and when two of his fingers rubbed my soaking wet clit I yelped with pleasure.

"Close, but not really. I'm just a desperate male with very talented hands."

"Anything else I should know about?"

"I have two cocks and one of them vibrates."

I balked, my jaw dropping in astonishment. How could he never have said anything?

Quillon's eyes sparkled like meteorite dust. "I'm kidding. But I have been told I am a fine specimen of the male physique."

"You're a bastard." I kissed him and ran my hands over his flesh, sighing at the beauty of the light brown muscle that rippled under my touch.

"And you're soaked," he said, dragging his fingers along the drenched seam of my core. "Have you been saving this all for me?"

"Yes," I whispered, aching. And then he plunged a finger into me. No, two. Pumping into the heat of my body, while another finger played with the swollen bead now addicted to his touch. My orgasm built in a matter of minutes, intensifying with every thrust of his hands. He maintained the most perfect pace, the most delicious pressure, never faltering until I was crying out with relief and sweet pleasure.

Before I could recover, he swept my legs around his waist and strolled down to my bedroom. There was no light to shine his way, but he knew the direction. He'd spent many nights beside me. But tonight he would finally get to tuck my body up against his. Skin to skin.

He gently placed me onto the bed, his gaze devouring my bare breasts, and with a smile that made my stomach clench, he went about lighting the candles along my bedside table. Once the room was bathed in a gentle yellow hue, he stalked over to the bed, a starved beast of a man ready to dig into his first meal in years.

"You're fucking beautiful you know that?" He climbed over my body, kissing me softly. "It was such torture seeing you upset and not being able to properly comfort you."

My heart melted and remoulded itself into the shape of his face. "But you did, Quillon, more than anyone has ever before." He filled up the empty bucket of my life with fresh hope and twinkling joy and being in his arms now was making it overflow.

He kissed me again, cupping my cheek and bringing our faces aligned so his nose connected with mine. "Aluma, I want to make you happy."

"I am now. So happy," I whispered, tears building behind my eyes.

"No. Not just for tonight. I want to make you happy for the rest of your life," he rested his forehead on mine and we both were quiet in the aftermath of his statement.

The tears that had gathered finally cascaded down the bridge of my nose. I clung to Quillon as if he was the only thing I needed to survive this wretched life. My beacon of light in a world that had wrecked me beyond measure.

I wanted to correct him about his earlier statement. I wasn't the gift. He was. And I planned on savouring it for as long as possible.

I kissed him again, gripping his huge biceps as he rolled his body on top of me. He moaned deep into my mouth, and I swallowed it up greedily.

Pulling away from me, he kissed his way down my bare stomach, pausing at the open buttons of my jeans to lick the exposed skin. He peeled my pants and my underwear down to my knees, shucked them off my ankles and flung them across the room. I laughed as he spread my legs wide and smiled. And then I wasn't laughing anymore. I was dying.

He licked his tongue square up the centre of me and my body spasmed at the contact. His hand reached up to grip my swollen breast, while the other pinched my thighs. I was bucking and whimpering as he focused all his attention on bringing me the deepest pleasure I had ever experienced. "You taste so *good*," he said against my wetness, thrusting his tongue inside me. I reached for his hair, his shoulders, trying to grab hold of anything while my body soared above the bed. I came with his name on my lips, and his lips on me.

"Okay, that's two for me. It's my turn now," I said, pulling him up and flat onto the bed beneath my eager hands. I clamped onto his length and stroked him softly, quickly casting my attention at the heap of black curls around his cock and then up at the swirling clouds in his grey eyes.

"Fuck," he said, and my skin blazed with a boost of confidence. I kept pumping him until I grew hungry for the taste of him. I shuffled down the bed until my head was resting above his tip. I made direct eye contact with him again as I licked him with my tongue and then covered him with my mouth.

"Yes," he breathed, every muscle in his body taught and trembling. "Aluma." I loved the sound of my name rolling from his lips. I loved the way his body reacted to what I was doing.

I loved *him*.

I could feel his cock pulsing and throbbing. He was close, it was obvious from the way he moaned and gripped the bed. But right before I was sure he would come, he sat up and reached for me. In one fluid motion I was on my back and he was poised above me. "If I come inside you Aluma, your body absorbs my essence."

"And?"

"And? I cannot stay here; I must go back. You would have to come with me, and I am not going to force you. Your life has been ravaged by too many men already." I traced the skin along his chest, my fingers gliding along a string of scars. Rugged and thick. Exactly how my soul had felt before he came along and smoothed it out.

I met his gaze. "But not by you. You saved me." I kissed him gently. "Do it. Make me yours," I wrapped my legs around his hips. "But how do *you* become *mine*? Is this just a one-way, misogynistic thing?"

He laughed and I felt his cock bounce between my legs. "I must ingest your blood, Aluma. Then we are bound."

I clasped my fingers around his neck and brought him close to my mouth so he could hear me when I whispered, "Then *bite* me."

Quillon crushed his lips to mine, sweeping his tongue inside my mouth at the same time his cock thrust into me with one hard push. I cried out and then wiggled as he paused so he could fit better inside me. Once seated, he moved his heavy hips and tight ass, working my body into a frenzy.

"Don't stop."

"I won't. I love you too much to ever stop." He slowed his lethal thrusts to look me in the eyes.

"Really?"

"Yes," he pressed his lips against my neck, my heart. "And I'm going to make you happy. I swear it."

We kissed. Delicately, sweetly. Then hungry and greedy. The metal cuffs on our wrists banged together as we found each other's hands and with each beautiful contact of his body against mine, they slowly started to loosen.

I never wanted this to end. I never wanted to leave the warm embrace of his love.

As Quillon began to grunt and tremble, and my orgasm unfurled like a shimmering veil, I bit the inside of my cheek, and slapped my mouth to his.

Blood spilled onto his tongue as he poured himself into me. We climaxed together, two beings from two different dimensions finding comfort in each other's arms.

He held me against him, his eyes blazing with something so deep it had no name.

"Are you ready to go?"

I stuttered. "What, now?" He picked me up into his arms, my thighs encircling his hips. "We're naked." I chuckled, laughter and love surrounding me in a bubble of stars. He kissed me again and again until we were both breathless.

"And that's how we'll remain for a very long time." And then we both brought the cuffs to our chests and pressed the button to release them.

To release *us*.

My world flipped instantly, but with Quillon holding me tight, it didn't matter where we went, because he would be there, and I would always be wanted and safe.

And happy.

12

LOST AND FOUND

K.E. TURNER

N athalie De Lancret eyed the security guard approaching her along the fence line. Backpack over her shoulder, camera in her hand, she looked like any other tourist. Behind her, nestled amongst manicured gardens filled with sightseers, the imposing fifteenth-century Château towered above the peaked roofs of Langeais. Pretty, picturesque. She barely spared them a glance, her focus fixed on the tenth-century ruins beyond the fence. She was here for a lot more than photographs.

Tucked in her bag was the newspaper article she'd received in the mail. A plain envelope, no return address, postmarked Paris. *Archaeologists set to uncover bones of 10th Century Chevalier*, the headline proclaimed. A knight, Gaharet d'Louncrais, was supposed to have died here. Could it be the key to unravelling the mystery of her birth parents?

D'Louncrais, De Lancret. Pronounced the same. Spelled differently. Could it be? Had the authorities got it wrong all those years back? She was only three when they'd found her, wandering alone in the forest at Landes, but she'd known her name. Nathalie De Lancret.

Was it a simple case of misspelling? Landes was five hundred kilometres away. She'd never extended her search this far. Years of investigating, finding nothing. Had she been looking in the wrong place? Could she be about to discover who she was, where she'd come from, and why the hell she could shift into a wolf?

The guard drew near and she raised her camera like a good tourist, snapping off pictures of crumbling keep walls.

"When will this be open again?" she asked, as he stopped beside her. She didn't look at him, pretending to focus her lens, taking a few more photos. But she felt him. The man had presence. She inhaled, taking in his scent. Musky, male. Her wolf shifted within, responding with an awareness that puzzled her.

"Months. Years. Not today."

Nathalie glanced at him, a polite smile ready. It stalled on her lips as she caught his gaze — hungry, predatory. Her inner wolf went berserk. What the hell? The need to shift burned within her. She tamped it down. She'd go for a run later, somewhere out of town. A wolf slinking through Langeais would attract attention.

The security guard looked her up and down, his nostrils flaring. Indignation spiked. She raised her chin a little and returned the favour. All lean muscle, he exuded strength and power. Sandy hair pulled back in a man bun, brown eyes like burnt caramel, a smile curving the corner of generous lips. Butterflies did the mamba in her stomach. Nathalie shook her head, turning back to the ruins. She wasn't here to scope out the local men. Although... a delicious shiver ran up her spine.

She raised her camera again, shooting off a few more photos. "Shame. I would've liked to see the ruins. Maybe even talk to the archaeologists. I think they're trying to find one of my ancestors."

"Is that so?"

Did she imagine the tension in his voice? Sometimes her wolf senses picked up things she didn't. She let her camera dangle around her neck, turning her attention to him. "I'm a De Lancret."

His eyes widened a fraction. His surprise fleeting, he shook his head and grinned. "Sure you are. You and a hundred others who want access to the site. Nice try, sweetheart."

Nathalie's lip curled. She was no one's sweetheart. She could turn into a wolf, for crying out loud. He wouldn't think her sweet then.

"I am a De Lancret. I'll prove it." She reached for her wallet to show him her licence, hoping he wouldn't call her bluff. Her research on the d'Louncrais had yielded nothing, not here, not anywhere. If she couldn't access the site, she'd have to follow one of the archaeologists to their hotel.

He folded his arms across his chest. "You could be related to the King of France and I still wouldn't let you in."

"France hasn't had a king since the French revolution."

"I know."

From the firm set of his lips, she wouldn't be getting past this guy today.

"No harm in trying." With a shrug and a smile, she retreated down the hill, the back of her neck tingling. If her wolf senses were anything to go by, he'd fixed his gaze on her arse. She glanced over her shoulder. He stood, hands on his hips, watching her. She hid her smile, gave a toss of her long hair, and exaggerated the swing of her hips. Maybe tomorrow she'd have better luck. She'd flirt with him to get what she wanted.

Dusk settled over Langeais as Laurent Voclain finished his shift. Slipping into his jacket, he reached for his phone. One message, from his brother.

> 'No d'Louncrais registered at any hotel in Langeais. Found a Nathalie De Lancret at Hotel le Roches. Coincidence? She used her credit card. She's not trying to hide. Can't find a birth record. She's in the system, though. Foster kid. Drives an '89 red Peugeot.'

Laurent shoved his phone in his pocket. She wasn't the first, and she wouldn't be the last to claim that name, trying to gain access to the excavation. She was, however, the only one who shared a common trait with the d'Louncrais. Her scent didn't lie. She was a werewolf, too.

He shoved his helmet on, threw his leg over his black Ducati, and started her up. A satisfying growl rumbled from her exhaust. She was a beautiful machine — sleek, powerful, fast, and almost animal. Like him. A ride on his baby would usually be enough to keep his wolf happy — the feel of the wind, the lean into the corners, the roar of the engine beneath him. Not tonight. He'd need more, a shift to the real animal inside. The dark-haired woman, with her bewitching green eyes — traits also common in the d'Louncrais line — had his wolf stirred up in ways he'd never felt before. Tonight, only a full shift and a run would satisfy him. It would have to wait.

Laurent peeled away from the kerb heading for the Hotel le Roches. Who was she? Why was she here? The d'Louncrais line had ended with the murder of Jean-Luc and his family, but... Could it be? Had their child survived? His pack had found no trace of Jean-Luc's three-year-old daughter all those years ago. They'd scoured the entire region for months. No sign, no sighting, no child found abandoned, lost, wandering alone. They'd presumed her dead. They'd enemies enough, seeking to uncover their identities, to destroy them, eradication of his kind their goal. Why spare the child?

As he approached the hotel, a battered, red Peugeot pulled into traffic. Staying a few cars back, he followed her out of town towards the woods behind the Chateau de Cremille. She turned into the parking lot at the head of the hiking trail, and he sped past, giving her ample time to leave her car before doing a u-turn.

He pulled into the parking lot, his headlight picking up the now empty Peugeot. He swung off his bike, removed his helmet, and strode over to the car. The thing was a rust bucket, one service away from the junk heap. He eyed the woods — dark, silent, a breeze rustling the leaves of old oak trees. Had her wolf, like his, needed a run after their encounter? He followed her scent to a pile of clothes folded in the hollow of a large tree. Grinning, he found himself a grassy spot, propped his back against a tree and awaited her return.

 C3&O

Nathalie stretched out her legs, enjoying the wind in her dark fur and the forest floor beneath her paws. A damp, earthy scent filled her lungs and the scuffling of nocturnal animals reached her ears. She'd come to relish this — the freedom, the thrill, the power in her body, her heightened senses. It hadn't always been this way. Her first shift had terrified her.

Alone and frightened, she'd huddled in her bedroom, not wanting to give another set of foster parents a reason to reject her. Now, ten years later, her wolf was as much a part of her as breathing. Even if she didn't understand everything her enhanced senses were telling her. Why did the security guard have her all hot and agitated? She'd never reacted to a man that way before.

Something about his scent tugged at her awareness, a sense of familiarity she couldn't place. Nathalie shook her furry head. It didn't matter. *He* didn't matter. She'd tracked down the hotel the archaeologists were staying at. A friendly chat with a young girl in the gift shop was all it took. She'd left a message with their hotel front desk, hoping they'd see her. Give her a few minutes of their time. She'd try the polite way first, but she wasn't leaving until she'd spoken to them.

Feeling better, a plan in place, her earlier agitation reduced to a low hum, she retraced her steps to her car. With each step closer, her unease grew. She caught a whiff of a scent. She paused. Raising her nose, she sniffed the air. No, it couldn't be. She drew in a deeper breath, slinking forward until she could see the trailhead. She stopped, flattened herself to the ground. His back against the tree, looking straight at her, sat the damn security guard.

What the hell?

She eyed him, all hot and sexy in biker's leathers. Beside his feet, the neat little pile of her clothes.

Shit.

Why was he here? Had he followed her? While she didn't mind the view, not at all, she couldn't stay here all night. Hidden in darkness, she waited. He didn't seem in any hurry to leave. What did he want?

"You can come on out now. I know you're there. I can see you," he called out.

What?

He couldn't possibly — His scent tickled her nose, musky, all male and a hint of... wolf? Her pulse raced. Could he be like her? She'd never met another person who could shift into a wolf. She'd often wondered if there were others; if her parents had the same ability.

He stood, picking up her clothes and tossed them toward her. She snarled, slinking backwards. Should she trust him? Reveal herself?

"I see you need a little convincing."

He slipped off his jacket, and before it hit the ground, he part shifted, his shirt ripping, bones contorting, fur sprouting. He stood before her, half human, half wolf.

Holy Mary, mother of God.

Blood roared in her ears.

Slinking forward, her eyes never leaving him, she snatched up her clothes in her jaws and darted behind a large tree. Willing the change, she returned to human form and dressed. Could he give her the answers she craved? Taking a deep breath, she stepped out from behind the tree.

He'd shifted back to fully human. Her heart skipped a beat, her lungs sucked in cool night air and she swallowed hard, her wolf going into overdrive.

So much for her run taking the edge off.

He stood, legs clad in snug, black leather, muscled chest bare, the shreds of his shirt at his feet. Sandy hair, long and tousled, brushed broad shoulders. She wanted to fan her face, relieve some of the heat spreading across her cheeks. Her gaze clung to his pecs, then dropped to his abs. The guy was seriously toned.

She licked her lips, her wolf threatening to bust out, take over and jump him right there on the forest floor. She clenched her fists to her side; her nails digging into her palms. A low rumble emanated from his chest, and her gaze flicked to his face. Hunger swirled in the depths of his eyes. Her face heated even further and her thighs clenched, dampness coating her panties. She'd never had such a visceral reaction to a man before.

He sniffed the air.

Oh good lord. He could smell her arousal.

She shut her eyes, blocking out the sight of his bare chest, but his scent, heady and intoxicating, invaded her nostrils, sinking in to the pores of her skin. She concentrated on her breathing. In, out. In, out. When she'd regained some measure of control, she opened her eyes.

Oh shit!

He'd moved so close she could touch him. She took a step back, holding her arm out to prevent him following. He stepped into her hand, her nerve endings firing to life as her palm connected with the heat of his skin. She bit back a moan.

"Who... who are you?" Her demand came out more like a husky invitation.

"I'm Laurent. Laurent Voclain. The big question is... who are you?"

Nathalie chewed the inside of her cheek. "Nathalie De Lancret."

"You think you're a relation to the d'Louncrais' of Langeais?"

His eyes fixed on her lips, his hand covered hers on his chest, halting the gentle brushing of her fingers against his skin.

Oh God. She'd caressed him. She hadn't meant to.

His hand tightened around hers. "So, do you?"

"What?"

Hell. She couldn't even think straight.

"Do you think you're related to the d'Louncrais' of Langeais?"

"Oh. Uhm... I... I don't know. I'm an orphan. All I have is a name and..." Her whole body quivered as he stepped in closer, her hand clasped in his between them, the only thing preventing their bodies from touching. "Are they like me, like... us?"

He grinned, his gaze molten heat flicking between her lips and her eyes. "Oh, yeah. The d'Louncrais came from a long line of werewolves."

Excitement pulsed through her. Had she found a connection to her parents?

"There's none of them left now."

Disappointment burned.

"Not since Jean-Luc and his wife were murdered." He paused, locking eyes with her. "Unless their daughter survived."

Nathalie's heart pounded. Caused by his words or from the closeness of his body, she couldn't tell.

His hand snaked around her neck, pulling her closer, his warm breath feathering across her lips. She should ask more questions, about this Jean-Luc and his daughter, the d'Louncrais, about him, but all her focus was on his lips, and how she wanted them against hers, kissing her.

She was so close to discovering the mystery of her birth, and — *Oh hell.*

He took her mouth in his, and she didn't pull away. God help her, she pressed herself against his naked chest, his tight leathers, the evidence of his arousal crushed between them. She opened her mouth on a sigh, inviting him in, and he didn't hesitate. His tongue slipped between her lips, tangling with hers. A large hand moved from her neck to palm her arse. The other tugged at her shirt, slipping beneath it and cupping her breast.

Her hands weren't passive either, tracing the contours of his back, her body on sensory overload. A deft twist and the front clasp of her bra released, his warm palm kneading her naked breast, rolling her nipple between his fingers. She moaned, arching against him. He growled, his hand moving to the button of her jeans.

Crack. The sharp sound split the air, forcing them apart. What the...?

ᚼᚱᚼᚱ

"Fuck!"

Laurent ducked as two more gunshots pierced the silence, splintering bark off a nearby tree. Nathalie shrieked. Grabbing her hand, he pulled her towards the parking lot.

"Is someone *shooting* at us?"

"Yes." He gritted his teeth, bursting from the questionable cover of the trees and into the open, heading straight for his bike.

"What about my car?"

"Forget your car. We don't have time." He swung his leg over his bike, tossing his helmet to her. "Hop on."

"But..." Another shot rang out, closer. They both ducked. Their shooter was a shit shot. He kicked the stand up, turned the key, pressed the ignition and the engine roared to life. "Get on the damn bike, Nathalie."

Green eyes wide she shoved the helmet on and swung her leg over, perching precariously behind him. He reached for her hands, securing them around his waist, glad of her werewolf strength.

"Hold on tight." He revved the throttle, and they skidded onto the bitumen in a spray of gravel.

Not needing the headlight to see, he used the darkness to their advantage. Fuck. How had they found him? Or had they traced her? KAE had a large reach, with many prominent and wealthy supporters willing to aid their cause. They'd targeted his kind, and others, for centuries, and were most likely responsible for the death of the d'Louncrais. Had they spared Nathalie as means of tracking them? Followed her, hoping she'd cross their paths, draw them out into the open? If so, their plan had worked.

Fuck. Why hadn't he scented them? Too wrapped up in her, that's why. He glanced in his side mirror. Headlights gained on them. Laurent opened the throttle further. Nathalie's arms tightened around him, pressing her breasts flush against his naked back. His cock just about punched through his zipper. He gritted his teeth. Bloody hell. He would have taken her on the forest floor if not for the interruption. Never had a woman, wolf or otherwise, affected him so. Made him feel like a teenager, all hormones and a raging erection.

Another check in his mirror. He grinned. A car couldn't keep pace with his baby. She was a beast, built for racing, a well-oiled machine. The lights of Langeais flickered in the distance. He would lose their tail amongst the streets, zipping in and out of the laneways as only a bike could.

He entered Langeais, hitting close to a hundred and seventy kilometres an hour. Any faster and he risked Nathalie being ripped off the bike by the force of the wind. He braked, bringing his speed down, leaning into the corner. Nathalie's grip tightened, but she leaned with him. Good girl. The next street, he turned left. Two streets down, a right.

A squeal of tyres and the sound of an engine revving followed them, but the car was falling behind. The roar of the Ducati's engine echoed off brick buildings as he zigzagged through the streets. He opened her up on a long straight stretch, weaving through traffic, before ducking into a lane. He spotted two trucks parked close together and slowed. A car couldn't pass them, the street was too narrow. Pulling to a stop, he reversed his bike between them, blocking them from view from either end of the lane. Cutting the engine, he turned to Nathalie and held a finger to his lips.

A car engine idled nearby, a beam of light skipping down the lane, touching buildings, cars, reflecting off the truck's side mirrors, but they remained hidden in the shadows. The car moved on, but would probably double back, check the other end of the lane. Starting his bike, keeping the revs down, the engine at a low rumble, he manoeuvred them out of their hiding place. Easing out of the lane, he weaved his way through the streets, keeping a constant lookout. Merging into traffic, he slotted in behind another bike, crossing over the Loire River on the Pont de Langeais.

Leaving the road, Laurent steered them beneath the bridge. Blue light from the pylons reflected on the water, the arches a shimmering gold, but they remained invisible in the bridge's shadows. Shutting down the engine, he kicked out the stand. Nathalie scampered off the back, pulling his helmet off.

"What the hell was that? People were shooting at us?" She trembled, her lip quivering.

"Hey, hey, hey." He swung his leg over the bike and gathered her in his arms. "It's okay."

She wrenched herself away.

"No. It's not *okay*. Why were people shooting at us? I mean, we were just standing there—" She flushed.

Laurent suppressed a grin. They weren't *just* standing there. In a few more seconds he'd have had his hand down her panties, his fingers sliding through her slick folds. His nostrils flared, the heady scent of her arousal still fresh in his mind.

"We were in human form. We weren't trespassing. And then they chased us. In their *car*!"

He stepped closer again, grabbing her hands in his, squeezing them, rubbing his thumb over her soft skin, soothing her. A tremor raced through her, her eyes glazing over.

Fuck. He'd never loved and hated his werewolf senses more than he did now.

The metallic scent of her fear was overlaid with the sweet scent of her lust. She licked her lips and his cock responded.

Focus. Answers first.

"KAE. They were KAE."

"KA who?"

"Kramerians Against Evil."

Her brows furrowed, confusion sparking in her expressive eyes.

"I know. Stupid name. They get it from Heinrich Kramer, the author of Malleus Maleficarum."

She gave him a blank look.

"The Hammer of Witches. The book which impacted the 16th and 17th century witch trials."

"Right. What's that got to do with us? With me?"

"Even before Kramer wrote the book, his ancestors hunted us, and any other creature deemed to have supernatural powers. Now it's not only his descendants. KAE membership has widened to include anyone wanting to rid the world of beings with inhuman powers. They're determined to stamp out anything they view as evil. That includes us."

"They must have seen us shift, but... how did they know we'd be there? I hadn't planned on a run." She frowned. "Did you follow me?"

"Yes. From your hotel."

She gaped at him.

"You were easy to find. You used your credit card. And I think I'm not the only one with that idea. It's possible they're using you to get to us."

"Someone sent me a newspaper article about the excavation. That's why I came. It's the first clue I've had to who my parents were."

He nodded. "Twenty-three years ago, the KAE murdered Jean-Luc, Fleur d'Louncrais and, we thought, their three-year-old daughter, Nathalie. The pack searched for you, scoured the entire Orleans Forest looking for signs of you."

"But I wasn't anywhere near there. I was found at Landes."

"That may be, but there's no doubt in my mind who you are." No doubt that he wanted her too, but he could wait.

He gritted his teeth. He would wait.

ৎৎৎ

Nathalie sucked in a breath. The gentle motion of his thumbs against her skin sent heat straight to her throbbing clit. She clenched her thighs. Bloody hell. The answers to every question she'd ever had were at hand, and all she could think about was stripping this man naked and riding him right here in the dirt beneath the Pont de Langeais. Or on his bike — that beautiful, sleek, rumbly machine that seemed an extension of his body as they'd sped through the streets of Langeais.

Heat flared in his eyes, but he stepped back.

"Come. I'll take you to see the pack. There are people who knew your parents well. They can answer all your questions, and I'm sure they'll have a few for you, too."

He strode to his bike and swung his leg over. "Jump on."

"What about my car?"

He shook his head. "Too dangerous to go back there now. We'll probably ditch it. The thing's a death trap, anyway."

"It's all I have."

He grinned. "Not anymore. You're one of us now. We take care of our own."

Warmth spread through her chest. She'd never belonged anywhere. Not really. A long list of foster placements made it difficult to form connections. Once she'd shifted, she'd resisted forming friendships even more, too afraid they'd discover her secret ability.

He held his hand out to her. "Come."

She eyed him — his muscular, leather-clad thighs, his bare torso, brown eyes promising to fulfil all her desires. She wasn't shy about asking for what she wanted. Foster care taught her those who didn't speak up, missed out. She licked her lips. He'd take her to meet others like her. There'd be introductions, questions, explanations. Lots and lots of talking. She didn't think he'd drop her and run, not with that look in his eyes, but... The moonlight, the lights from the bridge reflecting off the river, and his enticing scent inflamed the need that pulsed within her. It almost had her on her knees.

She wanted answers, but right now, she wanted him more. Before she could second guess herself, she ditched the helmet and jumped on the bike. Facing him, her legs hooked over his thighs. A deep growl rumbled in his throat and he grabbed her, pulling her tight against him. Their lips met in a frenzy of breathless hunger.

She clung to him, hands shaking with the fierceness of her desire, wanting to touch him, caress him, hold him. Cool night air brushed her skin as he peeled off her top, her bra already undone, quick to follow. He laid her back, arching her over the fuel tank, an arm behind her preventing her from connecting with the hot metal.

His eyes burned a path over her bare skin, and her nipples pebbled.

"You're so beautiful."

He dipped his head, sucking her nipple into his mouth, pinching it between his teeth. She gasped, clasping her hands in his hair, rocking her hips against the thick bar of his erection. The button on her jeans gave way to his fingers. Down went her zipper. Impatient fingers pushed aside her underwear and found her core, rubbing at her entrance.

Her hands fumbled at his fly. "I need... I want—" Her words ended in a moan as he inserted a finger inside her. She clenched her internal muscles around him and he growled. A shiver raced through her, a hint of what was to come.

"I need you naked, Nathalie." His voice was hoarse, his breath hot on her nipple, moist from his mouth.

He slipped his finger out, grabbing her waist band, struggling with her jeans. His bike wobbled.

"Fuck."

He gripped her tight around the waist, and she wrapped her legs around him. Lifting her, he swung his leg over his bike. Striding to a patch of grass, he lay her down, tugging her jeans over her hips and off, making quick work of her panties. He stripped off his leathers.

Nathalie's eyes widened. His cock thrust out, large and proud. She loved the confidence of a guy who went commando.

"Condom?"

He cursed, dug into the pocket of his leathers, pulled out a small packet.

Confident to the max.

He sheathed himself, and reached for her, sealing their lips with a kiss full of dominance, power and hunger. He flipped her over, setting her on her hands and knees. A growl had her glancing over her shoulder. His eyes were fixed on her sex, his face taut with need.

She wiggled her hips. "What are you waiting for?"

His eyes burned. Her breath hitched. He moved behind her, notched at her entrance, and thrust.

Yes.

Nothing had ever felt so right as him filling her, taking her from behind, fucking her in the open beneath the Pont de Langeais. This man she barely knew. She pressed back into him, meeting his thrusts. His arm caged her ribs, pulling her flush to his chest, changing the angle. She panted, moans of encouragement spilling from her mouth as he pumped into her. The slapping of flesh against flesh mingled with the sound of water lapping at the riverbank and the clack, clack of cars crossing the bridge above them.

A tingle started in the base of her spine, the walls of her channel fluttering. His lips nuzzled the curve of her shoulder, the scrape of his teeth sending her closer to the edge. His fingers dipped to her clit and pinched. Her body spasmed, her climax bursting over her — powerful, consuming. She threw back her head and screamed. With one last thrust he stiffened, his roar echoing off the bridge pylons as he came inside her.

They collapsed on the grass and he pulled her into his arms, their chests heaving. She lay in the darkness, residual spikes of pleasure shooting through her body.

"What now?" she asked once she'd found her breath.

He chuckled.

"Now I take you to meet the pack."

"Mmm. So... do we... ah... make a big thing out of what just happened?"

"You mean the incredible sex?"

Nathalie grinned. "It was pretty good, wasn't it?"

"Pretty *good*?" He raised himself up on his elbow. "You've had better?"

"Weeell..." She chuckled at his frown. "No, I haven't, but... We've just met. You don't know anything about me. I didn't want to presume—"

He cupped her face. "I know you're a d'Louncrais and a werewolf. I know I want you. Again. So, presume away, Nathalie." He brushed his thumb over her cheek. "We'll take it slow. One day at a time. But I'm not going anywhere, and I plan to be doing what we just did many times over."

Nathalie's heart stuttered. "Okay, but—" She grimaced. He stiffened against her. "Maybe next time we can do it in a bed like the normal people do. This grass has prickles in it."

He laughed, kissing her on the tip of her nose. "Come on. Let's get on the road."

She dressed, shoved on his helmet and hopped on the bike behind him. The throaty rumble of the engine filled the quiet night as Laurent steered them onto the road. She wrapped her arms around his waist, leaning into him, and he opened up the throttle.

She'd awoken this morning alone in this world, lost and adrift. Now she had people like her, who would shelter her and protect her. She squeezed Laurent tighter. And a sexy wolf-man to guide her through the transition. The KAE may have taken her from her birthright, but they'd led her back to it. The road ahead was unknown and full of potential. She smiled, the warmth of Laurent's body seeping into hers. Today she'd been found in the best way possible.

SWEET TREATS

Want to try something a little sweeter?

Why not try our Sweet Treats Anthology?

SWEET TREATS 2022:
ICE CREAM

Sweet Treats anthologies can be purchased from Online
Retailers, and from the
Romance Writers of Australia store

https://romanceaustralia.com/shop/

COMING IN 2023

Spicy Bites

The theme for 2023 is

Silk

Find full details on the Romance Writers of Australia website

https://romanceaustralia.com/contests-overview/spicy-bites-anthology/

Previous Spicy Bites anthologies can be purchased from the Romance Writers of Australia store

https://romanceaustralia.com/shop/

ABOUT THE AUTHORS

Victoria Brown

Victoria Brown never imagined becoming a writer. Though she admits to penning the odd poem. The idea for a story sparked from a failed attempt at relaxation in a gonging tent. Busy with an accounting practice and family at the time, she tried to shove it aside. Only, it had other ideas.

When she retired, over a decade of dog-eared jottings evolved into her first manuscript. She hasn't stopped writing since and loves it.

Australia's beautiful countryside inspires her and often her characters. Women's challenges are her focus—with romance of course.

She's on Facebook as <u>Victoria Brown Writes</u>.

Louisa Duval

Louisa works in secondary education and is also a podcaster, a former radio journalist and marketing professional. She plots contemporary small-town romance novels by the fireplace, with a glass of local wine at her thirty-five acre property in Queensland's Granite Belt region with her family and a fat cattle dog - Kelpie cross. Her local rural fire brigade inspires her heroes and heroines. Louisa was published in the 2021 Sweet Treats RWA anthology and shortlisted for Queensland Writers Centre's Adaptable program in 2021.

Find Louisa on Facebook and Instagram, and online: https://louisaduval.com

Fiona M Marsden

Fiona M Marsden started as an avid reader. She was late in finding romance novels, but once found, they became an addiction. Considering she wrote poetry and stories from a young age, it was only logical that the next step would be to write her own romances. She writes a cross section of everything genre. She recently started writing rural romance reflecting her long years of country living in regional Australia. Fiona is a hybrid author with several independently published works and contracts with Escape Publishing and Tule Publishing.

Twitter & Instagram: @fionammarsden

Facebook Author Page:

https://www.facebook.com/PrincessFionaMarsden

Web: www.fionamarsden.com

Georgia Moore

Georgia Moore has been a lover of romantic fiction since she realised she read every book waiting for the romance storyline to appear. Georgia writes contemporary romances featuring strong friendships and food as a love language, and SFF stories with plenty of action and heat. Her writing has featured in RWA's 2020 and 2021 Sweet Treats anthologies, and the 2020 Spicy Bites anthology. When not consuming copious amounts of pop-culture, Georgia can be found attempting a new cake recipe, singing in a choir, or being overly competitive at board games.

Follow Georgia on Instagram, Twitter, Facebook and TikTok @GMooreWriter

DK Harris

My first attempt at writing a book was about my first love—horses. But this was no ordinary horse, he was from Alpha Centauri and could talk. I also illustrated this book. I learned the hard way, even at age 7, that my writing skills far outstripped my drawing. Growing up on a steady diet of romance novels and sci-fi and fantasy in a house where reading of all kinds was encouraged, I never tired of finding fabulous books in both Speculative Fiction and Romance genres, but none crossing over. I dreamed of the day when the alpha prince would not only get his princess but would get the chance to bring their relationship to the fore, making it a major plot line.

I decided to combine my two loves and write the books I wanted to read. I love writing both alpha and beta heroes, all of whom I torture and make fall to their knees before their heroines and beg for mercy.

Kristin Silk

Kristin Silk loves weaving words and worlds. She lives with her family and a small but squeaky, furry tyrant, Martha the guinea pig, who thinks she's alpha of the household. (We don't have the heart to correct her.)

Kristin has stories in Spicy Bites Masks, Leather and Denim anthologies and Sweet Treats Chocolate anthology. In 2020, she won the Valerie Parv award. It's her fourth year of writing while recovering from concussion. (One out of ten stars – Do not recommend.)

She writes fantasy, paranormal and contemporary romance. She can be found at KristinSilkWriter (Facebook), @kristin.silk (Instagram) and @SilkKristin (Twitter).

Jennifer Westgarth

Long ago, Jennifer's appetite for escapism fell in love with her propensity to control, well, *everything*, and an obsession for writing was born! Now wise enough to know control is as fictional as her stories, Jennifer adores the journeys her characters take her on.

A background spanning interior design, policing and tourism furnishes her with an array of comical, dramatic and heart-warming experiences to ignite her creativity. When she's not writing resumes for a living, Jennifer divides her time between raising three hellions with her hubby, resuscitating a 60s renovator's delight, and finally completing her debut novel, *The Vintner's Muse.*

Katrina Louise

Katrina Louise lives with a tall, dark, handsome husband, three blond, blue-eyed sons and a desexed tabby cat who is obstinately alpha. To celebrate her lack of a Y chromosome, she pens tales showcasing heroines sweeping heroes off their feet. Some of her earliest childhood memories include playing dress-ups with imaginary friends. When twenty years of working in the movie business sparked a passion for storytelling and character creation, her imaginings found their way onto the written page. At her happiest rousing readers' hearts, loins, and laughter, you can find her online at:

Website: https://www.katrinalouiseauthor.com

Facebook: https://www.facebook.com/KatrinaLouiseAuthor

Instagram: @katrinalouisewrites

Karen Lieversz

Karen Lieversz writes women's fiction and romance. She explores the darker side of human behaviour and relationships, weaving humour and heat into her stories whenever the characters demand it (which is most of the time). When Karen isn't at her laptop, you can find her hitting the dance floor with her husband or walking her crazy kelpie-cross through the bush. More details about Karen, including anthologies where her short stories are published, can be found on her website: www.karenlieversz.com.

Or connect with Karen on Instagram –

www.Instagram.com/karenlieversz/.

Bridget W Deen

Bridget W Deen is a Sydney born writer with a deep love of books filled with fantasy and romance. Having graduated from university with a Bachelor of Musical Theatre and a Grad Dip in Secondary Education, Bridget spent years performing, teaching and reading, until a new found love of writing stole all of her attention. Currently she is working on two novels with the goal to publish them in the near future. Messaging strangers about books is her favourite past time and she loves doing it through her Instagram - @bwdbooks or through her website - bridgetwdeen.com

K.E. Turner

K.E. Turner can't remember a time when she wasn't reading books and writing stories — often when she should've been paying attention in class or, later in life when she should've been doing housework. After chasing her own happy ever after and settling across country with her man, it was time she took her writing more seriously. With a love of the paranormal and a good mystery, she writes romantic suspense and paranormal romance. She shares her life with her husband, her two dogs, two cats and a multitude of farm animals on their farmstay in Western Australia. Find her at:

https://www.instagram.com/k.e.turnerauthor/ or

https://www.facebook.com/K.E.Turner.Author/